STRANGELY, INCREDIBLY GOOD

CAT AND GENE
BOOK ONE

HEATHER GRACE STEWART

Strangely, Incredibly Good
By Heather Grace Stewart

The Anniversary Edition
Copyright 2025 by Graceful Publications

I

Katherine 'Cat' Glamour, you need to snap out of this. You're a grown, most-of-the-time-mature, 38-year-old woman. But I think you've finally lost it. You've finally lost your mind.

I blink one more time to make sure he's really there. He stands about 5'11, with a tanned complexion, muscular build, and jet black hair. His sparkling green eyes would win my complete attention if not for his bright red gym shorts and cut thigh muscles. I keep blinking but can't take my eyes away from the elaborate Celtic tattoo on his right bicep.

Yup, my Wii Fit trainer has jumped out of my TV, and he's standing in my messy living room. There's a pile of unfolded laundry on the maroon sofa, a pile of unread newspapers by the glass top coffee table, and a Greek God by the Wii Fit machine.

I've got to stop meeting my sister for Cosmos at happy hour on Mondays. Clearly, I can't handle even one tiny, overpriced umbrella-drink anymore.

I drop the Wii Fit remote. The room starts spinning. Seeing cheesies and chocolate milk stains on my carpet, I really wish I'd cleaned. The 911 responders, or perhaps the nice straight-jacket people, are going to be coming any minute, and will think I'm a fat, middle-aged slob who lives with her grandmother. *Which, let's face it, Fat Cat, you are, you are — and that's probably never going to change.*

Tears well in the bottom of my eyes before everything fades to black.

MY DAY HAD STARTED like any other ordinary Monday.

"Mom! Mom! I can't find my pink hoop earrings, and the bus is coming any minute!"

I wanted to hop out of bed and help her, despite the disrespectful tone. Jenna is my first born, my baby-turned-18-year-old-fashionista, and I want to grab every moment I can with her before she moves out later this summer.

The problem was, I couldn't just hop out of bed. That would require energy, and a sense of hope.

Which would require losing all this extra weight. At this point, I am starting to wonder if that's even possible. They say it can be done, but I feel so hopeless, so down on myself, all the time. I just don't know where to start. It's like I'm frozen solid: an ice sculpture left on the Rideau Canal, and the people passing by don't realize I'm stuck here. If I can't find the motivation to fold laundry or read those newspapers, I certainly can't start making healthy meals and exercising. Besides, I can't even make gazpacho. Even after following every damn word in *Chatelaine*.

"Jenna, honey, I have no idea where you left them. See if Grandma can help you."

"Oh, fine then. Grandmaaa!" Jenna bolted out of my bedroom and headed to the basement. Then, Alyssa was at my door, hanging from the doorframe; her thin, beautiful, not-yet-womanly frame swinging back and forth with restless energy. She kicked up a foot and practically vaulted into my room.

"Don't forget I have my gymnastics class after school tomorrow, and Jenna has art. So you can pick us up at the gym at six-thirty."

"I haven't forgotten sweetie."

"And Aunt Cicily's picking us up today, right?

"Yes. I have to work tomorrow, so we thought you could stay the night at Cici's. You'll have more fun with your cousins." I trusted my older sister, Cici, with my kids more than myself at times. She was uber-organized, to the point of having cubby-holes in her mud room for my kids as well as hers, and everything labelled in her kitchen cupboards. I hated to admit it, but I couldn't cope without Cici's help, and her visits to my money pit, er, home.

"That'll be fun. Um, I was just wondering, when you come get me tomorrow night, I was wondering if you *had* to wear a t-shirt and sweatpants."

"I don't think much else is washed right now."

"You mean not much else fits." She saw how my face fell and immediately covered hers.

"Oh God, I'm so sorry, Mommy." She sat on the bed and took my hand. "I don't know why I said that."

Alyssa always said she didn't know why she said things. She didn't know why she felt things, she just did. My girl who just knows things and calls it like it is. God, I wish I were more like her. But then I wouldn't have married a dipshit of a man and had her and Jenna, my angels from above. Sometimes, you can't win.

I'll never forget that day when Alyssa was seven going on eight, and we were eating cereal together before school. Out of the blue, she said, "Mommy, do you see pictures in your head, and then a little later, they happen just as you saw them?" She went on to describe how a friend of hers came limping into class just as she'd envisioned it an hour before, before her classmate had fallen and twisted her ankle.

It was then I realized she had the gift of foresight, and she probably knew a lot more about what was going on in my head and heart than perhaps even I knew.

Somehow, that made me feel safe. It also made me feel a little anxious. *Can I do it? Can I lose this weight that hangs over me like a dark cloud every day, and be the mother I've always wanted to be? I've been given these girls as a gift. I don't want to let them down.*

I squeezed her hand firmly. "Because you're frustrated, Lyssa. I get it. I can't do much with you girls. You know I'm working on it. You know this. "

I gently tucked a long strand of her lovely chestnut hair – just my shade, but thicker and healthier – behind her ear so I could see her beautiful face. "I'm working on it, Lyssa."

"Kay. Bye. See you tomorrow." She quickly pecked my cheek and looked down, nervously brushing off her plaid skirt and tights, though there wasn't anything there to brush off, and got up to leave.

"For your sixteenth birthday, honey, that's my goal."

She's heard that before. How many times am I going to lie to them? To myself?

As Alyssa left my bedroom, I heard the front door slam. Jenna had left for school, and for the night, without even saying goodbye. I was failing as the

Mom and friend I'd always wanted to be to them, and I only had myself to blame.

———

As I SHUFFLED into the living room in my black boot-style slippers and leopard print flannel PJs, I heard Gram talking very loudly on the phone with her friend Pat, or so I assumed. Then I heard her slam down the phone. I made my way into the kitchen and found her muttering away to a frying pan on the stove.

"With all the advances in technology, you'd think they'd design a 'Leave-Me-The-Fuck Alone' button for people who annoy the hell outta you," she grumbled and sat down with her plate of food at the kitchen table. "It was an automated message from the girls' school. Some creepy robotic female voice telling us the correct procedure for dropping your kids off, so you won't mess with the buses. Jeezus. When I went to school, teachers and principals actually knew how to write letters. With sentences, and punctuation, and everything!"

"Gram. I told you, we can get call display."

"Naw, can't afford it. Don't want to talk to anyone anyway. Shouldn't even answer the phone. You want eggs?"

I nodded, sat down, and started fiddling with my fork. *Do I want eggs? Sure. Sure, and I'd also like to know how it came to be that I'm sitting here with my 91-year-old grandmother, we have a generation gap miles wide, and she's the only person in the whole world who sees me right now. Not my fat.*

"What's buggin' ya, hon?" Her sky blue eyes conveyed such depth, such warmth, but her raspy voice and bitter tone betrayed that. All everyone ever saw was a curmudgeonly old woman who had outlived her children, and become a burden to her eldest grandchild.

That's not the case, Gram. It's not. Your body may be frail, but your spirit is as strong as an ox. Hell, I'm more of a burden to you these days.

"I'm losing the girls. Because of my weight. Because I embarrass them at school. I'm losing them." I tried to wipe away the tears with my napkin, but they kept coming.

"Not really. It's only temporary. You'll win them back. Besides, body image isn't everything. Well yeah, it is to teenagers, it's all they see these days. Photoshopped bodies on their phones, in their faces. But your girls know better than that. Deep down, they know you're just getting your shit together. You'll win them back." She was at the dishwasher, loading it, because I never had the energy to bend like that.

91-years-old. Something's going to have to change, Cat. My parents are gone, and Gram's not going to live forever. You can't ask Jenna to stay home after graduation to help you bend and lift things. You can't ask her that.

"You think? You think love should be a competition?"

"Honey, don't ask me about love, but life is a competition – with yourself – and only the bravest and strongest survive."

"Yeah. I know what you mean."

"Bacon?"

"No. Cutting back."

I swirled my eggs around my plate in little circles. "Gram?"

"Yes, cupcake."

"Dieting isn't working by itself. You know I've been doing that for years, and I just can't get results. So, today's my first day at the gym."

"Well I think that's wonderful. Since Jimmy left, you haven't done a godamned thing to take care of yourself. Yet you do so much for your girls and me…"

"Oh, a little less since the pounds started creeping up…"

I was already overweight when I got married, and gained ten pounds almost immediately. I'm honestly not sure how I went from pudgy to overweight in a matter of years. I'd tried every Miracle Diet out there, but the only miracle that had come out of those efforts was my Amazing, Shrinking Bank Account. I felt like a fool for falling for so many of the oldest tricks in the marketing book, but it's not like those companies don't know what they're doing.

When you're large in today's society, you're not

only a target of ridicule; you're also a marketing target. Even the healthy lifestyle options didn't sell you the staying power you needed to possess, alongside the product. I could have bought 100 Slap Chops and all the vegetables in the infomercial, but I needed to find the self-love within to do the chopping every night; to stick with healthy eating. *Yeah, I read that in an Oprah magazine. I knew all the theories. Applying them? That was another matter.*

Gram was right. I stopped taking care of me a long time ago. Most of my overeating happened late at night, in bed, watching TV. Those were the nights I felt most alone, and started thinking about the failure of my marriage, and all the things we'd left unsaid. We never did talk about little Logan. We never did.

When I'm honest with myself, I realize the marriage was doomed from the start. It was doomed that night in June, after my first year of business college, when I went to Jimmy Fink's house after a cheap date at Burger King, drank way too many wine coolers, and slept with him. I thought he'd make me feel better. An instant fix. Instead, we had to get a lot older in an instant. Or, at least, I did. I got pregnant. All because I was suffering from overwhelming guilt over a tragic event I felt I'd caused.

"Cat? Cat. You going to be gone all day?"

I looked at Gram, blinked a couple times, and realized I'd been staring into space far too long. "Oh, God no, Gram, just this afternoon. I'm going to the

gym soon, then I'm picking up my paycheque at
Walmart and running a few errands. The girls are
going to Cici's after school."

"I've got bridge at Pat's this afternoon. See you
later then. Oh, and Cat?"

"Yeah?"

"Knock 'em dead at the gym. Kick those skinny-
assed gals right off the treadmill!"

Yeah, if I don't give myself a heart attack. Sure.

As soon as she left, I took my plate of food and
scraped both eggs and some soggy toast into the
garbage.

*Ugh. This is gross now. I'll grab one last donut at
Timmie's before I start this new routine. I can do this. But it's
baby steps. Baby steps.*

2

It had been an effort to get there. Our town of Christmas, Ontario, population 75,000, is in rural Ottawa, about 30 minutes west of downtown. I only had to drive 10 minutes from our place to get to the new gym off the highway, but I hated driving anywhere on a weekday morning. No one follows the rules of the road anymore, and common courtesy flew out the window when everyone started texting more than talking.

Finding parking in the lot of a popular new gym was hell, but undressing in the locker room was a fire pit dance with Ledusa, the Goddess of Self-Loathing.

I wish they didn't have mirrors on the wall opposite the lockers, Ledusa whispered in my ear. I took my shirt off, turned to sit on the bench to take off my pants, and caught a look at myself in the mirror. Long, chestnut-coloured hair fell down past my shoulders, but it didn't come close enough to cover the blubber that spilled out from the top of my too-tight bra. My blue-grey eyes were a cloud-covered sky; they looked so lonely, so hopeless. I cast them down to my legs. *Ugh. Cottage cheese galore. I should just go sit in someone's fridge.* I sighed deeply then quickly threw on an extra-large black t-shirt, my sweat pants, socks, and running shoes.

Ugh. I hate having to wear this size. I hate how society makes you feel that you are the size you wear. I hate you, fashion industry, with your tiny t-shirts that only fit small, starving boys.

Once dressed, I had to climb a tall set of stairs from the locker room to the workout room, which sent my legs into spasms.

The gym people and equipment smelled like a bunch of used towels crammed into a laundry hamper. But worse than that? They smelled of success. And contempt. For me. I felt it in their gazes. I couldn't look them in their eyes.

I'm sure some of the gym people had looked like me at one time, but as I scanned the room I couldn't find anyone who looked more than five pounds overweight. Some of them even had lattes in their hands. The Starbucks ones, with the chocolate shavings on top. They weren't counting calories. *Maybe they're just here because it's something they… do. Like brushing their teeth every day. Was this just a social club for them? Must be nice.*

What was I even doing here? I couldn't do this! The lump in my throat got bigger, and I found myself choking back tears. I turned to walk back down *those fucking stairs* and came face to face with a bouncy, beaming girl in her mid-twenties.

"Leaving so soon? Maybe I can help?"

"No. I'm a lost cause."

"Oh no! Have you been set up with a trainer yet?"

"No, I don't need a trainer."

"Oh, I think you do. You really, really do." She had a clipboard in her hands. I guess she thought it was cute to whack me on my ass with it. I should have sued her for sexual harassment, but I didn't have the energy after those stairs.

"No, thanks, I really, really don't. And also? Your gym stinks."

Twenty minutes later, I was back at the Timmie's drive-thru, ordering a box of Timbits, telling myself Gram and the kids would help me with them.

———

I'D BEEN PLEASED NOT to run into any of my Walmart coworkers when I picked up my paycheque at my manager's office. Tom, my manager, gave me a smile when he handed me the envelope and told me he'd been happy with my work that month. If Tom thought getting my photo enlarged to an 11 by 13 and pinned to the break room's 'Employee of the Month' bulletin board was my greatest aspiration, boy, did he have me pegged wrong. I didn't want my photo tagged on Facebook, and I certainly didn't want it posted in public. Still, I smiled back and told him I'd see him tomorrow.

The costly mistake I often made when picking up my pay was turning toward the shopping aisle instead of heading back to my car and driving home. This time was no exception. I just wanted to feel a little Shopping Happy, that's all. What harm could looking do?

Cathy Hollows.

Quite simply, the meanest bitch I ever had to deal with in high school.

I probably still had icing sugar on my upper lip when she walked up to me. I was standing in the lingerie section, holding up the biggest, ugliest, purple lace panties you can imagine.

Quick, someone find me a hole.

"Cat? Is that you? I hardly recognized you!"

Stab number one.

I could feel Cathy's dark brown eyes picking me apart, piece by piece. I imagined her at a high-society cocktail party that night. Perfect little black dress and heels, flipping her straight, long, black hair over one shoulder, scrunching up that freckled nose as she laughed hysterically with her friends about our Walmart reunion – a child amused at her own joke.

Only, I was the joke, and she was having a great time repeating it as often as she could.

I remembered the first time I felt the prying eyes of thin people on me. I was fourteen, and I'd been invited to a high school pool party. I was thrilled to actually be invited, because I was far from the coolest girl in school. I wasn't on any high school teams, mostly because of the blubber on my butt and thighs. I was the chubby girl.

The two guys hosting the party, Jake Hampton and Jimmy Fink, had planned it for when Jimmy's parents were away in Bermuda. Little did I know I'd been invited to the pool party as a form of entertainment.

The reason I knew this is I (stupidly) married Jimmy Fink five years later. One day, in a drunken rage, he told me. "You need to get off your fat ass and clean up around here. Fat Cat. Yeah. Fat Cat. Do you remember when we started calling you that?"

"We?" I asked, blinking back the tears.

"Yes, we. Back in grade seven. That party? We wanted Fat Cat there to keep things fun. We had bets on whether you'd do a cannonball into the pool or not. You did. Too bad we never got that on vid. Oh. Wait. We *did*! Talk about making waves!" He started laughing so hard, he forgot he'd been angry, and about to hit me with the back of his hand. Instead, the beating hand went down to the coffee table, to a half-empty beer bottle. He took a few swigs and walked out of the room.

I'd been lying on the sofa, finishing off a Coke and a bag of chips at the end of a particularly stressful day. I was unable to get up after I learned my own husband had spawned the nickname that followed me all the way to my first year of college, when I'd dropped out to marry him. I lay there pretending to sleep until he left the house to go hang out at the local bar, and then I cried myself to sleep.

That party had been the day I met Ben Coverdrive. Ben. Beautiful, loving Ben. He'd stood up for me when everyone else was laughing, after I'd cannonballed into the pool. I thought the cool kids viewed me as funny and cool for doing so. But they'd planned it. They'd planned on watching my blubber wobble up and down as I bounced on the diving board, preparing to jump. They'd planned on gathering by the pool to capture it on video. This was the days before cell phone capture, thank God, but I later learned they still had it on tape and replayed it at all their parties. Just for kicks.

"Purple lace, huh?"

Cathy startled me back to reality. *Oh. My. God. She'd seen the panties.* I quickly tossed them in a bin to my side, then swept a hair from my face to try to look more presentable. *Why the hell do you care, Cat, she'll always look down on you, no matter what you do. Always.*

"Hey, Cathy. How have you been?"

"S*u-perrb*," she rolled the first syllable on her tongue like it was an appetizer, and drew out the last part like a box of fine chocolates. That was Cathy. She had to make a big entrance, a big exit, while making everyone in her way feel small and inferior.

"I was just on my way to my spin class, and I thought I'd pick up some bottled water." Innocent enough, but then she dropped the bomb. "Hey. Do you ever hear from Ben's parents? Or Logan's parents?"

Why would she bring that up? Why? She knew it was painful for me. The lump in my throat felt like a ball and a chain, pulling me deeper and deeper into the living hell I'd found myself in for twenty years.

"No. I don't think they want to hear from me."

"Oh of course, it was such a tragedy. Such a tragedy... The love of your life... A tragedy."

She shook her head back and forth like a teacher scolding a child, Tsk Tsk. I could see her eyeing some blue nail polish that was marked on sale across the aisle.

Why was she even talking to me? Oh! Right! High school reunion. Here it comes….

"Reunion's tomorrow! I'm so excited. You'll be there, of course?"

Oh let's see. You all call me Fat Cat, none of you have ever liked me, and you feel sorry that I lost the love of my life in high school, but you want to make sure I attend a reunion so you can all berate me in some bouncy dress?

I stood there, in the panties' section of Walmart, opened my mouth, and began to tell her that hell would have to freeze over before I could find the courage to show up this fat and unhappy to my high school reunion. Instead, I told her I'd be there.

"Be there or be square!" I laughed. *Oy. That was lame. Once a geek, always a geek.*

She got a very weird look on her face. "Oh. – I – Wow. Okay then, I guess we will see you there!" She walked over to the display of blue nail polish, grabbed a bottle, and smiled. "Now I just have to find the perfect dress to go with this for the reunion." She winked at me. "I've been searching retail stores for months, but with just a few hours left, I think I'll call up my designer friend and have her custom-make one for me. Good luck with yours!"

Bitch.

I held back the tears. I was not going to be that grown woman crying in the underwear section of Walmart. No. I was more than that. I would go to the candy section and cry there.

I was standing in front of rows and rows of beautiful, brightly coloured jube jubes and Mike and Ikes, just letting the tears stream down my face like a waterfall, when I remembered I needed to get bread, milk, and a variety of veggies so I could try making a healthy stir-fry tonight. *If I'm not sticking with the gym, at least I need to try making healthier meals for myself.*

As I WALKED out into the Walmart parking lot with a cart full of fresh produce in canvas bags, it started to rain. Just my luck. At least it was a summer rain, so it was cooling my skin. I decided not to run, because I knew that I couldn't without losing all my breath and dignity, but I made the most of it, and kept on walking and humming in the rain. *Ba dum dum dum, da dum, ba dum dum dum… I'm singing in the rain'…* It was exhilarating, knowing I was beginning a new chapter of my life, and the world was giving me a shower to celebrate.

Then I saw people staring at me as they ran from their cars to the store. Staring and frowning at me. Not even staring me in my eyes, more like at my stomach and thighs. A little boy pointed, and I saw his mother cover up his mouth, still running. Running, staring, pointing. *Just walk on past, Cat, just walk on past, you can't let their judgment stop you. You are going to lose this weight. So walk on past.*

I wasn't sure if the water I was licking from the corner of my mouth was rain, or tears. I tried to breathe deeply, to hold back from crying, but once I got to the car and lifted the bags into the trunk, I lowered my head, and the tears rushed from me, like water at a dam site.

I drove home, sadness streaming down my face. It was hard to see through the pouring rain and my tears. The more impaired my vision grew, the more nervous I felt that I'd rear-end someone. The last thing I needed was some angry driver shooting me over road rage. *I'm starting a new lifestyle. One day soon, I'll feel fabulous. No one is going to shoot me dead. Not today!*

This was too much. I was all turned around, and I couldn't see. I had to pull over. As I slowed down, two neon, lime green yard sale signs grabbed my attention on the right. They were wet, windblown, and practically illegible, but they did the job in helping me find a driveway I could pull into. I turned off the car, wiped my face off with the bottom of my shirt, and got out. I had to get my bearings.

I was looking down the street, trying to figure out where I'd made a wrong turn, when a man who looked like he was in his late sixties came over with an umbrella, and placed it over my head. Tall and slender, he was wearing a red lumberjack shirt and dark jeans.

"Rough weather, ain't it? Sure picked the wrong afternoon for a yard sale."

"It seems you did." I smiled politely. I just wanted to get back in the car.

"Have a look around my garage while you dry off." He motioned for me to take shelter in his double-car garage, which contained three tables-full of what would be another woman's treasures. Not mine. Not today.

Wait. Is that a Wii Fit machine? For twenty bucks?

I walked over to the table on the right and inspected the box.

Looks like this Wii is just $20, and it doesn't seem to have anything wrong with it, except that it's covered in dust.

"What's wrong with it?" I cut to the chase.

He didn't appear alarmed by my bluntness. "Never used it. My daughter brought it home when she moved here from L.A., but forgot about it in the garage. Now she's moved out, and we have no use for it."

I didn't hesitate. "I'll take it," I said, handing him my last twenty.

I needed to start working out in the comfort of my own home. Cici had told me the new Wii Fit was a lot of fun, and that I could even hook it up to the Internet, and watch Netflix movies on it. She'd left me her new disc. I could give it a try. Okay. This was great. I could do this.

The man carried the Wii to my trunk while, to my surprise, still holding the umbrella over my head with his other hand. *Huh. There are still true gentlemen left in this world.*

"Thank you," I said as I got in the car. "I hope it works."

"Sure. You'll see. It'll work like magic." He smiled and waved me on my way.

It was still raining as I made my way home, but I managed to pull safely into the garage. Then I just sat there. I didn't even know where to begin. I was going to look like a fool doing these exercises. But Gram wasn't home, which meant I could look ridiculous this first time and not have to listen to her making quips. Even if she meant well, meant to make me laugh, I couldn't bear it today. Not after running into Cathy and being reminded of Ben.

I hooked the Wii up to the TV as per the instructions, inserted Cici's new disc, poured a glass of water, and stood in front of our big screen, prepared to take on the world, or at least, the Wii, for an hour.

The Wii start screen came on.

<READY TO BEGIN?>

I pressed OK. The screen showed a computer generated man and a computer generated woman – rather cartoonish if you asked me – each of them wearing white t-shirts and red shorts.

<CHOOSE YOUR TRAINER>

Ok, that guy is pretty damn cute. Look at those muscles. I guess he'll motivate me. I certainly wouldn't trust him. But he'll be good for a workout.

I pointed my remote at the male trainer and hit

<SELECT>

Nothing happened. I shook the remote. Nothing happened. I shook it again. Nope. This was getting exhausting. I was about to give up my workout entirely.

I got down on the floor and did what any sane woman in my situation would do. I banged the hell out of the Wii box with the palm of my hand.

"*Listen to me, you fucking thing! Listen to me!*" I shouted.

I wasn't prepared for what happened next.

"*Your wish is my command!*"

It was a male trainer's voice, but it wasn't coming from the TV. It came from right in front of me; its echo, filling the entire living room.

I jumped up from the floor and looked up at the vision before me. No. He wasn't an apparition. He was a real man, dressed in real gym clothes. I raised my eyes ever so slowly. Abs of steel. A little bit of chin stubble. Charming, boyish smile.

He was grinning at me. This had to be bad news.

"You freak! Get out of my house! Get out, or I'll call the police!" I screamed.

"I'm not here to hurt you. I'm here to help you," the man from my Wii answered.

"Get out! Get out! Get out!"

That's when the room started spinning, and everything faded to black.

3

"Are you okay? Can I get you some water? Hey! Come on, you need to get up!"

I feel a gentle hand squeezing my left shoulder, and the soothing warmth of a wet cloth on my forehead. I open my eyes. They're met with a striking pair of piercing green eyes and a kind, boyish smile.

"Hi there. I didn't mean to frighten you. This always happens!"

I blink. He's still there. I rise up slowly to a sitting position. He's still there.

"You make women pass out a lot?"

"Yes, and you know, I'm pretty fed up with women fainting when I'm only trying to do my job here."

"*Oh*, so you're doing me a favour by appearing out of nowhere?"

"As a matter of fact, I am! Look, I'm sorry I

scared you, okay, but I haven't figured out how to make the entrance work yet."

"Entrance? Work? You fucking appeared from out of my Wii machine! I'm not sure that could ever... *work*!"

"Listen." He sits at the end of the sofa. I sense he is trying to create trust by not sitting in my personal space. There's no way I am trusting something that came out of my Wii machine, but at this point, I figure I've fallen and hit my head really hard. Any time now, I'm going to wake up, and the nice hospital people are going to let me push a little button to receive morphine whenever my mistaken little brain desires it. So, I may as well just sit here and see what happens next.

"I used to come out of bottles, and lamps. But there aren't many of those around anymore, except in antique shops," he says.

I think my mouth may actually be wide open right now. I don't say anything; just let him continue.

"I needed to be found sooner than every 20 years. The world is changing, and I had to adapt. Maybe I should have gone with Apple. An iPad. Maybe an iPhone. Yeah. Damn it, I need to be put back in an iPhone next time..."

Oh, for God's sake. Wii guy is mumbling to himself. This is not what I wanted from this day.

"Wait a second. You're trying to convince me you're from some other world, and you live inside computer chips, but you're a real dude?" I cough, and he taps me on the back.

"As real as you. Living, breathing, feeling. I just have a different definition of home. I have to." I notice his shoulders slumping, like he has silently sighed.

"Huh?" I crawl to the other side of the sofa, pull myself up, and fall back into it. I need its comfort to get me through this surreal conversation.

No, I can't sit near him right now. I have to leave the room. That's it. I'll leave, and when I come back, Dude from my Wii won't be there anymore. That's how it happens in the movies, right? Okay then.

I get up, walk to the bathroom, and look in the mirror. Yup, that's me, and I'm not hooked up to an IV or anything. I'm standing here looking into my blue-grey eyes, debating if I should call 911 or not. *I remember Ben once compared my eyes to the bottom of a swamp. He swore this was an attempt at romance, but I was PMSing, so the 'romance' ended with a banana split on top of his head.* The eyes looking back at me look sane. I mean as sane as I'll ever be. *So, do I call 911?*

I decide to go look at him again. He really doesn't *look* like a mass murderer, but what do they look like, anyway, if they're not wearing a white hockey mask? I peek my head around the doorframe. Just my head.

He's still sitting at the far end of the sofa.

"Let me try to explain this to you," he calls over to me. "Er, what's your name?"

I don't know what to say. This guy is acting like he does this every day. I just stand against the doorframe and stare at him. He stares back. I guess I'm going to have to respond.

"Katherine. Friends call me Cat. Who are you?"

He takes a deep breath and exhales. "I'm a genie. I was born in Greece and lived like any other man does, until one day, everything changed. I've been under a sorcerer's spell since 326 BC. I was cast aside for hundreds of years in old lamps, but my most recent Master didn't like where my magic got her. So, she had a case of road rage without the road, or the car. She wished me into her Wii machine, which was thrown out, then wound up being recycled in a series of yard sales. That's how you found me."

"Sure. And I'm the Dali Lama."

Genie nut job is staring at me intently. He looks amused. Yes, his mouth is creeping upwards into a smile.

"Look. I know in your world everything is black and white, but magic isn't like that, Cat. Magic is a rainbow. How do you describe a rainbow to someone who's never seen one before?" He sighs deeply, and mutters something under his breath that I can't quite make out. Something like, "here we go again."

I look back into those piercing green eyes, then lower my gaze downward to his strong hands and bulging calf muscles.

How can someone so entirely delicious be so royally loopdy loop? It's such a shame.

"Okay." I inhale and exhale in one breath. "So you're… what's your name?"

"It's Eugenius. It's a Latin-based name that…"

"Eugenius? Sure, because you're a genie. Clever. Your delusions are actually clever! Okay Eugenius, that's a mouthful, so I'm gonna have to call you Eugene. That okay with you?"

He nods, then stands and asks, "Hey, Katherine, I was wondering, do you have any breakfast foods I could partake in? Perhaps a croissant? I've been locked away inside that Wii for years. I'm famished."

I gather all the energy I have left to get up and start walking around my living room in a circle, slowly, very slowly.

How come I haven't woken up in the hospital yet? This is really happening? Holy hell. This is really happening.

There's a genie of my Wii in my living room. Demanding croissants.

Maybe I had a massive heart attack in Walmart after seeing Cathy, and I blacked out, and don't remember any of it. Maybe I'm already in my hospital bed, and that morphine is coursing through my veins, causing me to hallucinate. There has to be a logical explanation for all this. I'm going to have to ask questions. Maybe he'll answer me better if I feed him.

I walk to the kitchen and find a large bowl of cheesies on the counter. How old are these? Right, last night. I snacked on them when everyone else was asleep. Fine. These'll do.

When I turn around, there he is, doing side bends for some reason, but still grinning at me rather awkwardly.

"*Eugene!*" I jump, and several cheesies spill out from the bowl. I catch my breath. "You can't keep startling me like this."

"I'm sorry, I thought maybe you could use a hand in here." He stops his exercising, takes the cheesie bowl from me, leans up against the counter, and begins munching on them.

"These are awful for you, you know." He holds up a cheesie, carefully inspecting it. "I can't believe you eat this crap. I lived on a farm when I was a boy, and one of my chores was making cheese. This is not even remotely close to how that tasted. This is so full of artificial, I think it could fly to Mars, visit the surface in one of those fancy rovers, return to Earth, and still look and taste the same as it did the year before."

I decide to ignore that tirade and focus on the larger problem in my life right now.

"Alright, Eugene, let's say you're actually under a spell. It led you to have genie qualities. If that's true, how come I don't see or hear about the work of genies in the world today?"

"Ah. You don't see genie magic? How do you explain those Kardashian sisters?"

"Huh? They used your magic?"

"Yes, but not very well. You have to be careful what you wish for. You only get three wishes, and there are rules. Kim wished for a flawless wedding, not a flawless marriage. It lasted seventy-two days, and on that seventy-second day, she banished me to her Wii as her third wish. She was so angry. I tried my best to move to a bigger living space, from the Wii to the Internet, but before I could, she had her assistant throw it out. She had her assistant do everything for her, even buy her underwear. No joke."

"Huh. So, people don't always use you wisely."

"Not always. Take Donald Trump. He never asked for great hair. He asked for great wealth."

I can't help but chuckle at that one. He chuckles back, and I immediately frown. I can't let him see me letting down my guard.

"You've been to Trump's tower?"

"Master, I *built* Trump's tower." He chuckles, and puts the bowl of cheesies down. "All of his Entertainment Resorts too. But I can't reveal any more of my clients' wishes. I shouldn't have revealed as much as I have. I just... I want you to believe."

"I don't believe it, but I do believe this: You have to stop calling me Master. I'm not going to order you around and tie you up to my bed. This isn't Fifty Shades of Genie." I laugh at my own joke. He's not laughing. Alright. Ancient Greek boy doesn't get the reference.

"Can I call you Katherine? I truly love that name. It suits you more than Cat. It's classy. You're classy," he says, and I notice he's munching away on the cheesies again. Hypocrite. See, I knew I could find a flaw or two in this guy to combat his perfectly chiselled chin and haunting eyes.

"Seriously? Okay, then, I guess," I say as I pull up a chair at the kitchen table and sit down. "So, tell me, when you say 'your wish is my command,' what do you mean by that?"

Eugene pulls up a chair as well, and I try to digest what he has to say next. "Katherine. You are my Master. You get three wishes. And you have as long as you want to use those three wishes. I will stay with you until they're all granted."

"You've got to be kidding me." I laugh, a little at first, but then it comes rolling out of me like a little kid playing in the waves, piquing with tiny, high utterances of pure amusement. "You're just some homeless dude looking for a place to stay!"

He lowers his gaze to the table and takes a deep breath. When he looks up, I see his face has fallen to an emotion I hadn't yet seen. Oh. He's hurt.

"Oh for the love of God, Katherine!" he slams down the bowl of cheesies on the counter, hard. Then he inhales deeply; exhales loudly. "You women I try to help. You all question me. You are all broken, so you all question if I'm the real deal. Well I am. I'm a real man, but I'm trapped in a cycle I can't get out of. I don't know how to make you see. I don't think you even care, so I'm not even going to bother. Just send me back to the Wii. Please." He pushes his chair back, gets up from the table, and walks away.

"*Ooooh!* I've pissed off the Genie of my Wiiiiiiiiiiiiiiii! I hope he doesn't put a hex on me!" I call after him, giggling.

To my surprise, I don't hear an answer.

4

A FEW MOMENTS PASS IN SILENCE.

Then I hear two distinct sounds.

SLAM! Is that Eugene leaving?

"Hiya! Take that, you vile beast!"

Oh. Okay, no, that's Gram. Shit. Oh Shit!

I push myself off my chair as fast as I can using my hands as levers on the table, but by the time I've done that and made it from the kitchen to the living room, Eugene is lying on the floor in the fetal position, writhing in pain.

"It's okay. I'll be okay. Ack." He's still curled up, massaging his pelvic area. "It's not like I have a normal life anyway. Didn't think I'd get any kind of action here any time soon."

Gram is standing above him with one leg in the air, arms raised above her head, like Ralph Macchio in *The Karate Kid*. Only, with a metal cane.

"There you go, darlin'. I kicked the sucker in the family jewels. You called 911?"

"Gram. Gram! Stand-off. Seriously. He's okay. He's actually kind... just a little weird. He's... um. Um. My personal trainer, Gram. From the gym. They sent him home with me because I need so much help."

I catch Eugene looking up at me. His awkward smile turns into an outright grin. Is he for real? Can he really help me? *What* am I doing here? I'm inviting a stranger into our home, just because he's cute and can possibly grant me three wishes? This is completely nutso. How am I going to sell this to Gram? How am I going to explain this to the girls, and the neighbours?

And yet, something deep down in my gut tells me to go against my logic and better judgement, and keep this guy – this guy who's complaining that he has to stay here to help me – around. Did I have bad sushi last night? My gut must be completely off.

"How the hell can you afford that?" Gram lowers her foot, arms, and cane. Eugene looks relieved.

Ever since my ex left me with the text message, "I'm outta here," I've been struggling to pay for our next meal. I'm glad Jimmy's gone. In fact, I wish I'd been brave and strong enough to kick him out myself, but finding work after being a stay-at-home parent for over 15 years proved nearly impossible. The job I ended up getting isn't what I dreamed for myself back when I was in high school. I had planned on going to business school; on managing a business. Now I work at Walmart, ringing through other people's shiny new toys.

"Oh right, the money for it? The money for it. Yeah it's um… it's an experiment. They're doing this at the gym as a courtesy because they want to study – ah – fat chicks like me. Yeah. They want to learn what works best: a trainer in one's home environment, or at a gym. I'm being paid for his food and stuff. There's the futon in the basement so I thought…"

"We thought it would be a good arrangement," Eugene pipes in to help me.

"I don't know what you've been smoking, dearie, but I guess he can stay. He's nice to look at anyway." She looks down at him. "Sorry about your balls. My bad."

I'm stifling laughter, until I see Eugene is chuckling too. He slowly gets up and extends his hand. "That's alright, Ma'am. You were defending your turf. That's a good thing. I'm Eugenius… er, Eugene for short."

"You have a nice ass." She pinches his bottom as she passes him and starts to walk to the stairs; he jumps. He isn't laughing now.

"Gram! Don't be perverted," I call after her.

She turns on her heel and puts her hands on her hips. "Look, honey, I'm no pervert, just a Grandma who don't lie. Never faked it in my life. Maybe an extra "ooo baby," so I wouldn't miss Cheers."

Eugene and I look at each other and burst into laughter.

Gram doesn't look amused. "Fine, go on then, laugh. But don't think old people don't get horny. We just can't satisfy it as fast as you. We go out to get some, and forget where we live."

She doesn't stop to hear our reaction. She just continues on up the stairs. I glance at Eugene again and motion for him to sit on the couch. I sit first, and when he sits beside me, this time, he sits a little closer.

"I'm sorry about her. She's… she's a unique trip."

"That's an understatement."

I hesitate, then spurt out, "And I'm sorry, Eugene, but I still don't believe you. I don't feel like you're going to harm us in any way, but I seriously think you may need to see someone about this genie delusion of yours…"

"Oh right, right, this is the age of therapy." He scratches his chin stubble absentmindedly as he thinks. "I wish we'd had therapy in my time, when I was a free man. We dealt with our pain by building incredible cathedrals and amphitheatres so we could have ceremonies and shows to take our minds off the pain, I suppose."

"You honestly believe you're from another era?"

This guy is something else. The crazy part isn't that he thinks he's a genie. It's that I'm starting to trust him. Yeah. Something tells me I could definitely trust him. I don't want him to leave.

Wait, now. I've made this kind of mistake with men before. I always give them the benefit of the doubt and get in over my head way too fast. Before I know it, there are more 'doubts' about the guy than benefits. I know this probably stems from the abuse I took from Jimmy. I just want to be loved the way I deserve to be loved.

Then again, giving Gene a chance couldn't be any worse than going on the series of dates I went on in 2011, after Jimmy granted me our divorce. Those were complete nightmares.

I wasn't in the mood for love the year Jimmy finally left the house and Gram had moved in to keep me company. I wasn't even in the mood for 'just sex,' as Gram had so often suggested. She left me post-it-notes in weird places, as if they were only subtle hints. Exhibit A: The highly-anti-feminist hint atop the garbage can:

Getting close to time to take this out. Or you could invite a man over to help you. And then sleep with him. It'd take the edge off. ~Gram

I completely ignored that note and took out the garbage. Then, just to prove to Gram I didn't need a man around the house to do daily tasks anyone could do, I hung a new portrait of the girls all by myself (only bruised my thumbnail a little). Next, I made a point of refilling every single soap dispenser as I cleaned the bathrooms. *Am I the only human being alive who always spills the large soap refill when I'm trying to refill the soap dispensers? I eye it, think I've got it, then,*

Glugshhhlerp.

All over the place. So much for that "deal" on one litre of liquid soap. I know I need to buy a funnel for this sole purpose. Instead, I clean the sinks with the excess soap, and keep on buying the refills in the hopes that one day I will get it right. It's a lot like how my dating life turned out, only I never got sparkling clean sinks out of my lousy dates.

Gram persisted with those 'subtle' hints. Exhibit B: The dreadful poem stuck to my undies in my laundry hamper.

A little old lady knows you wear this zebra thong, go find a man, because that's just wrong.

That one actually made me laugh out loud, and then Gram and the girls came into my room and asked me if we could talk. A dating intervention? Seriously?

We all sat on my rickety Queen bed. Gram broke the uneasy silence first.

"We know it's been a real adjustment, living without the girls' father under this roof."

"Ding dong the Jerk is gone!" Alyssa interjected. Such a ham.

"Amen!" Jenna added.

"Jimmy finally leaving was like the villain being shot at the end of the movie," Gram said, "But it's been hard on you. We want to see you smiling again." She took my hand. I didn't know what to say. Gram was never mushy like this.

"Yeah, Mommy, we want you to go on *dates*!" Alyssa giggled.

"Really, Mom, it's okay if you do." Jenna rubbed little circles on the back of my waffle robe. "Just don't date any of my teachers, okay?"

I hadn't thought about that one, ever. Trust Jenna to conjure the image of me dating her teacher. I wrapped my arms around the leopard print pillow that had been behind me, and imagined what it might be like to dance with Jenna's handsome, 30-something third grade teacher, Lewis Lightfoot. That wasn't his real name, it was Mr. Lewis of course, but I liked to call him Lewis Lightfoot after word got around with the Moms in the class that Mr. Lewis was single and had won a Ballroom Dancing Competition that fall.

I emailed Mr. Lewis one October day that year to ask how many children were in the class. I'd been asked to bake something for the upcoming 'Breakfast with the Parents' event, and I wanted to make enough for everyone. However, in my hurry and excitement to get a third item checked off my parental list of Things That Never Ever Get Done, I accidentally addressed the email: 'Dear Mr. Lightfoot'.

I never told Jenna about this ridiculous error, and

in his reply he simply ignored the mistake, but I broke out into a sweat just thinking about the possibility of running into him at school. Ah yes, to my great embarrassment, Lewis Lightfoot became the principal of Trudeau High, my alma mater, where my girls go to school. Luckily, I have never run into him. I stay in the car almost every time I pick up the girls, now that I've gained so much weight. I haven't seen the school hallways, let alone his office. Still, I imagined what that might be like, if I were lighter, and if I had had time to put on jeans and a nice sweater, and do my makeup…

"Hello, Lewis, er, I mean, Mr. Lewis," I'd murmur in a low, seductive purr, after a quick knock on his open door.

"Cat?" Mr. Lewis would straighten his tie a little, then start to blush.

"Well, hello." I'd come in and close the door behind me. "What's a bad boy, like you doing in a place like this?"

"I don't know." He'd get up from his desk and come straight for me, placing his hands at my waist. "Maybe we should break some rules and find out," he'd say as he'd lean me up against his desk and kiss me, long and hard, full of pent up passion.

Geesh Cat, must your fantasies be so pathetically cheesy? *I'm not ready to date. I'm not ready to have to look nice. I actually like sweatpants. I'm not ready to have to sound interested in everything the guy has to say, just for the sake of getting a second date. I like debate. I like disagreeing with men!*

It makes life interesting. Above all else, I'm not ready for anyone to see me naked.

I stood up. "Thanks for the good wishes everyone. Girls, I think it's well past your bedtime! C'mon, go brush your teeth. Lyssa, did you study your French dictée words?"

Of course they meant well, but I would date when I was good and ready, and several pounds lighter.

5

As it turned out, Cici thought I was good and ready to jump back into the dating scene the very next week at Herb's Café, the artsy little spot where we loved to meet for Cosmos on Mondays. They had a great 2-for-1 at Happy Hour, and it had become a ritual for us to meet there once a week to catch up on each other's lives. Gram watched all the kids for us at Cici's place, which made the weekly date easier to manage.

I can still see every one of my dates, all so clearly, in my mind. Every last agonizing detail.

"Ooo, Cat! You're here!" Cici grinned as I hurried in from the rain, 15 minutes late, and headed to our regular table. My tall, redheaded sister stood to hug me, then motioned for me to sit beside someone. Some man.

No one ever joined us for our Cosmo dates. It was an unspoken rule. *She broke it!* I looked over at Sister Bonding Time Spoiling (SBTS) Guy. He was a nerdy kind of cute, in a navy business suit and matching striped tie, but still, I was going to kill my sister. I sat down and took his hand as he extended it.

"Cam. I'm Cameron, but everyone calls me Cam."

Okay. Enough already. What was the deal with this guy? I wanted to fast-forward to what was wrong with him, so I could end this surprise date, and get back home in my jammies.

"I'll leave you two alone." Cici left some money on the table, buttoned her coat, and kept her eyes on the floor. She knew what my reaction would be.

"What? We haven't even had drinks together. Look. It's all very nice to meet you, Sam—"

"Cam," SBTS Guy corrected me, adjusting his glasses.

"Sorry, Cam, but Cici, I didn't sign up for this."

Cam looked over at Cici, then started fiddling nervously with the stem of his glass of red wine.

"*Kath-er-ine.*" Her voice became higher pitched, and she enunciated every syllable of my name, like I'd always imagined our mother would, had she lived to raise us. Then she gave me that look she always gives me when she thinks she knows what's best for me.

"Just stay a while. Cam is an accountant. He works with Simon." Simon's her husband. "He's a good guy." Cam was smiling at his glass of wine. This was so awkward.

"Okay, bye," I said to a wall, and waved the waitress over. I watched Cici leave through the window, and tried to imagine what had been going through her head when she set this up.

"I'll have a Cosmo and Sam – Cam – here will have…" I decided to be polite. I also decided that since it appeared we were stuck together, even if just for the next half hour, I desperately needed a drink.

"I'm fine with this one, thanks." Cam looked up at the waitress.

Hmm, maybe I was being too hard on poor SBTS guy. It wasn't his fault Sister Bonding Time was spoiled. He had no idea he was only a pawn in one of my sister's many evil plots. *Cue eerie music.* Mwa ha ha ha…*oh right, stop daydreaming, better converse with the nice man. This is, after all, a date. I should do my best to get back on the horse, as they say. Or saddle. Damn. Which one is it?*

I looked over at the poor accountant guy. He'd had a long day, doing whatever accountants do, and he was probably dragged out on this date out of a sense of duty to his friend, Simon. Maybe he knew I was divorced, but had he expected the fat? Had they warned him? What would they have said? "Oh and by the way, Cam, she's a little on the plump side of plump?" I shuddered, thinking of the conversation. It made me want to curl up in a ball.

I needed to at least make a valiant effort. Cam seemed like a genuinely nice guy. Suit. Tie. He drank red wine, but only a glass at a time. Respectable.

"So, Cam. Have you lived in Christmas long?"

"Half my life. Moved here from the States when I was in my twenties."

"Oh, from where?"

"Oregon. Listen. I've done this before, and I've come to learn it's best to just get all the uncomfortable stuff out of the way."

"Oh, okay, sure, sure. What did you want to know?"

"How many more dates until sex?"

I choked on my Cosmo. Well, this was great. I was going to die of shock at Happy Hour. What a way to go. No one was going to save me in that very loud resto-bar, certainly not Can't-Wait-Cam.

"You okay?"

"No." I coughed into a napkin. "No, didn't see that coming." I got up and started rummaging through my purse for my wallet.

"Wait! Come on! I was half joking!" He chuckled awkwardly.

"Half joking? Oh, that's fine then, okay, then let's just go to bed and get that part over with."

"Seriously?" He grinned at me and started to get

up from the table. "Oh shit, I have my kids at my place right now." He ran his hand through his hair.

How did I ever think Can't-Wait-Cam was cute? His hair was greasy, and his smile was creepy. At this point, he was just a desperate guy in an expensive suit.

"Separate beds, Cam. We'll be in separate beds. Have a nice rest of the evening." I threw some cash on the table, turned and walked away.

What a perfectly good waste of Sister Bonding Time.

I DIDN'T THINK DATING COULD GO downhill after that. How much more hill was left at the bottom at that point, right?

Wrong.

Later that night, Cici apologized profusely by text.

> So sorry. Jeezus. Didn't know he was such a jerk. Forgive me? xo

> Know you meant well. Pls dnt bring anyone else 2 our Cosmo dates. Want to drink in misery of being old and fat with sister.

> Hey, I'm not fat! Or old! Bitch.

I laughed out loud. I could handle talking about my weight with her, and it was never a competition.

Though she was at a healthy weight, she'd been supportive – a participant, in fact – of all my attempts to lose weight, including the time I asked her to follow the latest craze and drink Spinach and Chick Pea Shakes with me for two whole weeks. She was such a sport, even buying the groceries for our little adventure, because I couldn't afford everything. Such a sport, until 3 p.m. on Day Three, when I received this text from her:

> In crucial business meeting. Boss making a presentation. Am filling up room with atrocious fart smell. Do I stay or do I leave?

> Be heroic. Tell them to get out while they're still breathing!

I put my phone down on the kitchen table, threw my head back, and had the biggest belly laugh I'd had in ages. Tears were streaming down my face. Then Gram came in.

"What's the joke?" She stood at the counter, making tea.

"Oh God, Cici and I have the farts. It appears these shakes make us fart."

"I coulda told you that. Shit Shakes. That's how they taste, and that's what they make you do."

"You think we're actually going to lose weight on these?" I pushed my half-empty green shake glass away, feeling a little nauseous.

"I think you're gonna poop a lot, get sick of the Shit Shakes, and fill up on all your favourite foods next week. That's what I think."

I wanted to laugh and cry at the same time.

"Yeah. I hate to say it, but you're probably… Ewww." I'd let another big one out. They just kept coming and coming. I'd lost all control!

"I'm outta here, Fartsy. You'd better get a handle on that before you bed another man." She raised her tea mug and nodded, as if to wish me luck.

Fart Attack (FA) was a passing (pardon the pun) scene in the Cici and Cat show. Luckily, the attacks subsided once we were out of ammunition, mainly because we listened to Gram, and stopped providing the fuel that was our Shit Shakes. We laughed about FA for months after that, but Cici had to get a job in another department, just to save face, and to stop hearing her co-workers whisper, "Poopsy" every time she walked past.

Perhaps Can't-Wait-Cam was a subconscious retaliation for the pain she'd endured during our FA period. Nevertheless, she remained loving and supportive long after FA and Can't-Wait-Cam. Perhaps too supportive, as she convinced me to try an online dating service so that I could "get myself out there," and meet men with similar tastes and hobbies.

HOBBIES? What the hell are my hobbies? Getting a full eight hours of sleep? A fight-free day with my daughters? No, those won't work. I was sitting at my computer, trying to fill out my form for the service Cici had suggested, *Until Death.*

If you asked me, *Until Death* was one morose company name, but they claimed on their home page to have a three-year success rate of 70 percent. I guessed that meant the couple didn't want to kill each other after three years, which was more than I could say for my marriage, so I figured I'd sign up and get everyone in my family off my case.

I ended up putting "Family activities" and "Rock climbing" down under Hobbies. I've never actually tried rock climbing, but I've always wanted to. This was good. This way, I was simply presenting myself as a single mom with an interest in spending time with her family, and showing my adventurous side as well.

Oh crap. I was just lying! I was sitting there, filling out that online dating form, eating a Mars Bar and ketchup chips, while my kids were playing with Gram in the backyard.

It pained me to think how much I'd lost because of my lack of self-confidence. I used to be so involved with my girls in the early years of my marriage. Of course, I'd had to be. I had to protect them from Jimmy's abuse. I was thankful he never harmed them physically, like he harmed me for so many years. But he did talk down to them, and make them feel guilty for things that weren't their fault. I used to have to keep on my toes to try to hide anything they'd done that 'little kids just do,' so that Jimmy wouldn't come home from the bar, find one of their creative messes, and go off on them for the entire night. His tantrums were so much worse than theirs ever were.

One night, he was so violent, I was sure he was going to turn the corner and start hitting the girls, too. They could hear his screaming, slapping, and my body being slammed against our bedroom door. Oh, their little ears, their innocent little minds, their pure spirits. I wish I could erase it all for them. All I could do that night was pack a bag for myself and one for the girls, and get out. I went to the cheapest motel I could find in our town, because it was so late, I didn't want to awaken Cici or Gram.

The room was a total dump. Dark, dingy; the Queen bed had questionable stains on the duvet, and cigarette butts were strewn across the floor from a fallen ashtray the maid failed to clean up. The girls checked the room out before I got my coat off and called out to me that they'd found a cockroach in the shower stall. Jenna wanted to name him 'Roachy.'

"Please, Mommy, can we keep Roachy as our pet? He's scary looking. Maybe he can protect us from Daddy!"

She always knew how to make me laugh when I was down in the dumps, but this time, I reacted quite differently. I sat on the toilet, head in hands, and cried and cried. The girls came and rubbed my back. I hated when I fell apart like that in front of them. I regained my composure quickly, drying my tears with my sleeve.

"Hey. How does Dairy Queen sound?" I tried to sound chipper.

"Isn't it past midnight?" Jenna asked. I looked at my watch. 12:03 a.m.

"Right. Right you are. Poutine? The Burger King drive-thru is always open!"

"But we're in our pajamas, Mommy," Alyssa said.

"So. Poutine Night in our PJs! Come on, it'll be fun!"

"Yay! Mommy! You're the best!" they squealed in unison as I grabbed the car keys, a blanket, and a stuffy for each of them.

Later that night, Poutine Night in our PJ's became Poop & Puke Night in our PJs, as all three of us came down with the flu, or food poisoning – I never had time to find out which it was. We spent 24 hours holed up in that hotel room, most of it in the bathroom. Turn by turn, I held their little heads over the toilet, rubbed their backs, pulled their beautiful hair back so it wouldn't get barf through it. Soon, the sick smell made me sick, and we found ourselves sitting around the toilet, waiting for whoever's turn it was next, from whichever end. It was not a pleasant evening, stuck with our backs against the toilet, but when the trips to the washroom finally eased up for us, we snuggled together in that Queen bed (minus the gross Duvet, which I'd stuffed in the closet), and played Flashlight Fairies on the Ceiling.

The game was a simple one I'd come up with at the spur of the moment, because I hadn't had time to grab any toys or books for the girls when I had rushed us out of the house that night. I had thought to bring my carry-on bag of toiletries and medicine, though, and gave them each a teaspoon of Pepto Bismal, and three for me.

"Look, girls! This room has flashlight fairies!" I gave them each a little flashlight I'd packed for them, and used the tiny one on my car keychain to show them what I meant. "See?" I said, relaxing into my pillow and feeling relieved I'd finally lost the urge to upchuck my poutine all over the place. I twirled the flashlight around and around, creating a dancing 'fairy' on the ceiling.

"Wow! Cool!" Jenna said, and her 'fairy' joined mine on the ceiling.

"Me too! Me too!" Alyssa cried out, and I heard her giggle for the first time that night. "Oh, maybe they're Illness Fairies, Mommy?" Jenna was so creative.

"Maybe they'll mageecally take our die-ah-ree-aa away!" Alyssa exclaimed.

Our fairies danced on that ceiling for over an hour that night, until the girls were overcome by exhaustion, and they finally dozed off. I watched them lying there peacefully, snuggled up against me, their arms outstretched above their heads like they were trying to fly. I wished they could always look so serene, as they climbed their mountains; the insurmountable challenges they'd face in their lives.

I WASN'T ALWAYS that calm and collected with my girls. No. Weekday mornings, getting them ready for the bus, always pushed my Patient Mommy Mask too far, and it eventually fell off, revealing my Mad Mommy Mask underneath. Oh, that wasn't a pretty mask at all.

When the girls were both in primary school, the bus would arrive just across the street at 7:33 every morning without fail, and sometimes a little earlier. It wasn't being a single mother that made our mornings challenging. It was simply that I was a parent getting them ready to go somewhere they didn't want to go. I wish every human being well in this particular segment of the parenting journey. You are a freaking *saint* if you're in charge of the morning routine and don't yell at your kid at least once a week. Or maybe you know about a brand of Ibuprofen, or strong, coffee that I have yet to discover.

One morning, everything was running smoothly. Too smoothly. I could smell spilled cereal, or kid barf, or forgotten homework around the corner, because nothing had gone wrong for the entire 43 minutes we'd been awake.

Then Alyssa came around the corner, into the kitchen, telling me she had to make a headband-crown-thingy and poppy for "'Membrance Day." It was 7:27am. She had only eaten half a banana, and her tights were bunching at her bum and falling down at her knees. She looked like Eeyore, only in red, which worked to her advantage when I told her, "No, there isn't time," because she sulked and moaned, "Oh, my life *so* isn't *fair!*"

I closed up her lunch bag, grabbed Jenna's lunch bag from the counter, and led Lyssa out of the kitchen into the living room, where her sister was putting on her shoes and coat. I pointed to Lyssa's shoes.

"It's not even Remembrance Day, honey. It's November eighth. I don't know why you need to have this headband and poppy *right this moment…*"

"But it is Mommy," Jenna interrupted. "See?"

Jenna pulled the School Calendar out of her backpack. Sure enough, the school was having their Remembrance Day Assembly on November eighth even though November eleventh fell on a Monday, a school day. This happened with so many school events. Perhaps it was a conspiracy. They had turned November eighth into Remembrance Day just to learn which parents could remain sane, and which ones belonged in an institution. I was sure this was why they did that. I would be marked 'Incapable' with a Permanent Sharpie, probably at the centre of my forehead, very, very soon.

"Lyssa, we have to get our shoes and coats on now. You'll miss the bus if we don't."

Lyssa looked at me and stomped her foot. "But I want to make a crown! *A Happy 'Membrance Day* crown. With a happy poppy on it!" she shouted.

"Lyssa, Remembrance Day is *not* freaking happy! It's a solemn occasion! Solemn! Do you know what that means?"

Her chin started to wobble. Oh no, and then there were tears. And the bus!

"Run, girls, *Leave your mitts! Leave your coats open! Just run, will youuuu!*" I yelled as we ran out the door, certain in that moment that every neighbour on my street was actually a School Spy, planted there to make sure I was doing a Capable Job. Surely, they were watching the girls run across the asphalt in tights, open coats, with their shoes dangling from their hands, instead of on their feet, as they ran to catch the bus. Surely, every single School Spy was marking "Incapable. Incompetent." on my Parent Report Card right that moment.

I felt awful the minute the bus door closed, and not only because I couldn't see the girls' faces behind those dark tinted windows (since when did school buses go all celebrity?), so I didn't know if they were smiling again or not, but also because I looked down at my feet and realized I was standing in socks, plaid

PJ bottoms, and a 'Too Sexy For This Shirt' t-shirt. Great. Definite 'F' in Parent Apparel.

I also felt awful that I'd not explained to Alyssa what Remembrance Day was all about. I thought I had, but surely, if the school had properly done their job, Lyssa wouldn't have considered it just one more Dollar Store Holiday? Maybe it wasn't anyone's fault, but the fault of society's crazy commercial tendencies. Since the time they could talk, my girls had been programmed that 'Happy St. Patrick's Day' hats and antennae (doesn't every Lucky boy or girl need green sparkly antennae?) came out in the stores in February; 'Happy Valentine's Day' banners by January first, Halloween horror arrived in stores in late summer, and of course 'Merry Christmas' everything came out October first, long before the day we honoured those who fought for our freedom.

After feeling awful about the Morning-Routine-Gone-Wrong all day while I worked an eight-hour shift behind the Customer Service desk (you would not believe some of the curses that come out of some peoples' mouths when they want their $2.98 back), I picked up Jenna and Lyssa at Cici's house. Both girls were beaming, holding a *"Membrance Day'* wreath, as Lyssa so cheerfully called it. We got in the car to drive home, and I heard all about their glorious day with no mention of them being scarred for life by the run to the bus that morning.

"We got to sing 'Oh, Canada', in front of dah

whole school," Lyssa said, clapping her hands. "It *was* a Happy 'Membrance day after all, Mommy!"

Pick your battles. That's what I've learned most from my years of parenting. Pick. Your. Battles. I kept quiet as I turned into our driveway that afternoon. Besides, Christmas was coming. I knew I'd best save my energy for the 'Great Christmas Commercial Overload', wherein my children were brainwashed every Saturday morning into thinking they desperately needed every single toy advertised, with each toy made in China, available only in the US, almost impossible to buy and ship to Canada, and always at the appallingly ridiculous price of $89.99 and over. Pick. Your. Battles.

————

DESPITE THE LATE NIGHTS, early mornings, puke, poop, and persistence that come hand in hand with parenting, I have fond memories of raising my little girls. I've certainly tried to make lemonade out of a life of lemons. I know in my heart that I'm trying to be a good Mom, but have I taught them everything they need to know before I set them out on their own, into this beautiful mess of a world?

I continued filling out my dating profile, but was distracted with worry. Had I done enough with the girls lately? *There's always an excuse as to why I can't take them to the movies, travel with them on summer vacation, or just take them out after school for ice cream. I should stop with the excuses. I'm capable of anything. I just needed to change my attitude. Gain back some confidence. Maybe dating would do that for me. Maybe I was on the right path. Maybe my date would even take me rock climbing!*

I saved the file, added a five-year-old head shot, pressed publish, and logged out of Until Death. I felt a surge of possibility race through my veins. It made me dizzy with excitement. *What was I feeling? Hope? God. I hadn't felt that in years.*

Hope died, *Ding Dong* the Hope was Gone, the moment I opened the door to meet Date #2, an environmental scientist named Evan.

———

It wasn't how he looked. Come on. On a good day, I call myself curvalicious, but backward modern medicine still calls me 'overweight.' I'm not going to judge anyone by how they look.

It was how he smelled. I couldn't put my finger on what that odour was, not even in the car, when I'd had to roll down a window, to force some fresh air in and the body odour out.

"Ah, you love fresh air too?" Enviro Evan looked away from the road a moment to look over at me, and grinned. "We must be a match made in heaven."

It wasn't until we were sitting down in the restaurant, sharing the bowl of salty chips and salsa the waiter had placed between us, when I finally recognized two of the three distinct smells coming from Enviro Evan's body. Vinegar. One was vinegar, and the other was definitely…

A strong citrus scent wafted past my nose. Lemons! Yes, and there was another aroma I couldn't yet make out. I decided I'd have to just ask. Surely he had a good explanation for how he smelled? An experiment perhaps? His profile claimed he'd won many awards in his field. Perhaps that was what this is all about: The pursuit of excellence in science. A worthy pursuit indeed! I was determined to remain positive about this.

I took a swig of red wine and blurted out, "What's with the smell? Vinegar and lemons?"

"Oh, you can smell that can you?" Enviro Evan chuckled. "I suppose it *is* rather strong." He took a sip of his Rooibos tea and smelled his own forearm, a little too long, in my opinion. Was he actually getting off on his own smell? I looked down at my menu, trying to hide how uncomfortable I was by nodding and smiling at every item I read. Already, two full tables of people across from us had whispered something to our waiter, gotten up, and moved away from the atrocious smell.

I had meant to come out and only order drinks, so I wouldn't blow my diet. Just a drink or two. But all I could think about was French onion soup. Hot, steaming, cheesy, French onion soup. Mmm. Could that possibly cover up Enviro Evan's smell? Maybe I'd order two bowls, then. And three or four warm, thick, buttery slices of bread to dip in the soup. Yes. That scent of fresh bread. I needed it. I needed it right then. *Fuck the diet. Bring me bread!*

"Cat, I need to confess something to you up front here."

Dear Lord in Heaven, help me. Was this going to be another case of Can't-Wait-Cam? Please, no, I thought. Please at least let me savour my French onion soup and fresh bread before this ended badly. Give me that.

I chuckled out loud. Confession time, huh? I couldn't help but think of the Lord's prayer we were taught to recite every morning when I was in primary school, and wondered if it was sacrilegious to pray to Him in that moment.

"Give me this date, my fresh hot bread, and forgive me my debts…"

No. Not especially socially acceptable. But who said I wanted to fit in?

"You're already laughing. You're supposed to wait to laugh, Cat."

I didn't realize I was laughing out loud. I smiled awkwardly at Enviro Guy and bit into another chip. "Go on. Confess."

"I don't bathe."

"Really?" I said with my best, false, incredulous tone, and, trying my best to avoid another bad-date-choking-incident, swallowed what was in my mouth before speaking again. "I would never know."

"Yeah, I mean you can't tell about the lemons unless you have a really strong nose, which I guess you do," he grinned.

I looked around the restaurant. It's like we were armed robbers in the middle of a bank, and we'd just announced a hold up. All the other couples in the room, seven in total, were squished at tables the waiter had set up in the far corner, against the wall. They were staring down at their plates, avoiding my gaze. *Oh shit!* Did they think we're a... thing? Yes. They thought I was *with* him with him. Perfect. Just perfect. Where was that soup and bread I ordered?

"I don't believe in soap."

"You don't believe in soap? Is that some kind of... religion?" I put my napkin to my mouth, feigned wiping my lips, and bit my left cheek to keep the laughter in.

"No, but I am what some could call an Environmental Kook. Me, I just feel like doing my part to save our planet." He took off his glasses, and placed his hand on mine. Had he done this shtick before? It felt premeditated. *Oh, yes, here it comes. He's going to sing to me.*

"I could be your hero, baby," he sang, softly, but off key. "I could save your Planet Earth." He chuckled, gazing into my eyes like it was the most romantic thing that had happened to me in years. Which, sad truth be told, it *was* way more romance than I'd received in years. *Help me. My life is a travesty.*

I stopped him before people started to get up. Too late. Couples three and five in the far corner were putting on their coats.

I pulled my hand away from Enviro Evan's grip, raised it like an eager first-grader, and was relieved when our waiter arrived at our table seconds later.

"Hey, I ordered two bowls of French Onion soup, a salad, and some bread? A while back?"

"It's just going to be one more minute, sorry for the delay." The waiter was, oddly enough, moving his shoulder up toward his nose. He was probably trying to cover up the stench while still holding plates and a notebook. His shoulder wouldn't reach his nose. *Good. You're in this with me, buddy. We all are. Prisoners of Evil Enviro Evan. Hey, at least you're getting paid to endure this complete violation of the freedom to breathe freely in a public place.*

Suddenly, I was craving lemon meringue pie. *Yes. Lemon meringue pie: that would hit the spot!* I ordered the entire pie in the dessert display by the front counter. "You can just wrap up what I don't eat, right?" I said, realizing it had been years since I ate so much in public. What the hell was wrong with me? Usually, I did my over-eating in private, or at least in my car in a parking lot, slouched down a little so no one could witness me and my bad habits.

Wait a minute. Onions! That was it! He smelled of onions, vinegar, and lemons. I ordered French onion soup, a salad with vinaigrette dressing, and an entire lemon meringue pie.

It was all his fault. It was how he smelled. He made me hungry! Evil Evan, Impenetrable Stench; Destroyer of Perfectly Good Diets.

I needed to get out of there. *But how? How? Too late.* The food had arrived. A delicious aroma filled the space before me. I couldn't resist it. I broke the steaming, fresh bread and shoved it hungrily into my mouth, relieved I had something else to concentrate on while Enviro Evan remained on his Soap Box, talking about soap.

"You don't know what one bar of soap can do. Paints, soaps, nail polish, and other chemicals harm the ocean life."

"I agree," I said, not wanting to sound like someone who was indifferent to his cause. "I just wonder…" I hesitated, then decided, someone had to tell him, and since I hopefully would never see him again, maybe offending him outright was the way to go. "I wonder if there's another product you can use that won't destroy our oceans. Perhaps a powerful, hard-working, organic soap?"

"Indeedy! That's what I use, Katherine! And the best part? I made it myself."

"Of course you did." I smiled and just gave up. I gave in to temptation. *Lemon pie, here I come. Ohh, that is scrumptious!*

After an hour of listening to Enviro Evan explain

what was in his soap, how he made it, and how he applied it to his body every third day, I couldn't take anymore. My plate was empty, and there was no longer any lovely aroma to help disguise his stench.

"This has been interesting, Evan, but my girls have school tomorrow, and I need to get home to make sure they're in bed."

"Right! Taking care of future generations! That's the ticket!" He grinned.

Did he just say, 'That's the ticket?'

He was very careful about calculations when our bill arrived: circled every item I ordered, and calculated my half of the tip. I'm all for equality, but this was ridiculous.

"Be sure to tell your girls about my soap," he said as he pulled up to the front of my house. "Maybe you can try it on them. Maybe they'll like it so much, the whole idea will go *viral*."

"Maybe," I said as I got out of the car. "You never know." I forced a smile and waved.

Five minutes after I got in the door and said hello to my girls and Gram, I rushed upstairs, tore off my Evil Evan infected clothes, and took a long, hot shower, practically making out with my mandarin-scented soap.

6

EUGENE TURNS HIS GAZE SO HE'S LOOKING DIRECTLY in my eyes again. "Katherine. Take my hands. Now. Trust me. You will believe soon. Look at me. Look at me and make a wish…"

Ding DONG.

Saved by the bell.

I get up and go to the door. I can see through the glass that it's my least favourite person in the world. Jimmy. My ex. Ex is an appropriate term. He looks like an ex-con: thin scar across his nose, fierce dark brown eyes, furrowed brow. Yet, his tattered jean jacket and converse high tops make him look like he's fresh out of high school. When he hit me, all 62″of him went into it. It's a wonder I'm still alive. I should have put a restraining order on him, but I was so afraid. Too afraid. *At least he never hit the girls.*

"Gram has been calling me, asking for help with

the girls. I don't want no trouble from the courts. Here's your fucking money, okay." He throws an envelope at my chest. It floats down to the floor, falling, falling, falling flat – as all my hopes did in the years we lived together.

"Listen. I know you have to work, so I wanna pick the girls up today and keep them for the weekend. I want them to meet someone. My girlfriend. I have a new girlfriend."

I blink. I wonder who the fool is who fell for him. He does still have the right to see his daughters, but I need to protect them.

"Sorry. We have other plans. They don't want to spend time with you, Jimmy. You know that. They don't trust you."

"God damnit!" He kicks his feet at a loose brick on our house. "I'm recovering. I'm in AA. They gotta give me a chance."

"So many chances, Jim…" I choke back the tears. I'm finding it hard to breathe. Now I can feel a hand on my shoulder behind me, but it doesn't startle me at all. This feels so comforting.

"Who's this schmuck?" Jimmy asks and motions to Eugene behind me.

"He's my trainer. I'm in training."

"Ha! Good luck with that." Jimmy laughs.

"Just go, Jimmy. Just go."

"Yeah, yeah, yeah. But I'll probably see you around Walmart, huh, checkout girl?" He laughs so hard he reveals the three broken teeth he got a couple years ago. I'd always wished it had been me who broke those teeth, but no, it was the steering wheel, or maybe the oak tree, that broke them, that time he hadn't come home for 24 hours. I still don't know where he'd been, he refused to talk about it, but he didn't need to. His breath and clothes told the story for me. He reeked of whiskey and dirty money and women, with not a scent of 'working overtime.'

"Yes, Jimmy. I'm a checkout *woman*. Only because I'm broke, and surprisingly, you're not. Your misguided parents pay for all your mistakes, and they bought you a house and a cook and a cleaner and God knows what else after our divorce. Like you were the wounded one. Who was the one who got thrown to the kitchen floor with a bloody nose all the time?"

He keeps looking at me with an expressionless face; completely remorse-free.

"Maybe your parents will keep cleaning up your messes, but I won't be anywhere near your messes. Not for long. I'm working on myself. How about you? You doing the same? Or will you drink the rest of your life away?"

I don't know how I'm finding the strength to talk back to him. It's this hand on my shoulder. I can't believe how powerful this one hand makes me feel. Could it be true? This one hand makes me feel like changing my entire life.

"And another thing. I'm not even going to work.

I'm taking a couple days off. " I'm not sure where the idea comes from, but I figure if I'm about to change my life, I'm not going to have the time to ring up other people's purchases in a dark blue uniform. I glance up at Eugene. Something flashes across his eyes. I've seen it before, in Gram's eyes, and in Cici's eyes: The badass protective gene. You don't cross them. Ever.

Jimmy gives me and Eugene a quizzical look, taking a moment to try to find words of retaliation, but when he opens his mouth, nothing comes out. He backs away and practically runs down the stairs.

Eugene has both hands on my shoulders now, and turns me around to face him.

"There. How did that feel?" He's got that awkward smile again. The one I'm starting to like. "You've never stood up to him before, have you?"

I shake my head 'no.' I walk into the living room and sit down. He sits close to me this time.

"So, how did that feel?"

I pause, let my body fall back into the soft sofa, and breathe out. He's waiting for my answer, but I just want to bask in this moment for a while longer.

"Strangely, incredibly good." I can feel tears of joy falling down my cheeks as I break into a grin.

"Yes, I know, and it's just the beginning, Katherine. Just the beginning."

Is this happening? Am I actually starting to believe this guy who came from my Wii, telling me he can make my dreams come true? Well, he's proven he's not dangerous, he definitely uses soap, and he's actually an interesting conversationalist. I guess I could play along. I don't have much to lose. Except a whole lot of weight.

I *want* to believe him. I *want* it to be a new start for me. But my mind has always preferred logic over fantasy. It's my natural tendency to think Cinderella would tumble ass-first down the castle stairs and break a leg, because she's running so fast in those tiny glass slippers.

I just need to know more about him first. "Tell me about your life in Ancient Greece. How do you not have culture shock here, if you lived in a time before cars, before the Internet, before… running shoes?"

"My life as a free man was short and uneventful. I've seen more as a genie than I ever did as a farmer in Greece. As a genie, I've been to sock hops and roller-skating rinks. I've seen the front lines of World War One, and people crying at the wall of missing people posters in the aftermath of nine-eleven. I've seen clothes go out of fashion; then come back in fashion. I've watched women's rights change drastically; from a time when women could be Pharaoh to not being considered citizens at all, to being Prime Minister of a country. I'm still waiting on President. Maybe you'll wish for that. Maybe I'll get to witness it with you as my Master."

"Oh, no, no, I'm not interested in being President!

Besides, I'm Canadian, remember?" I chuckle. "I just want to be thin, and to be loved again. Truly loved, like when I was a teen. Oh! Is that all I have to do then? To wish?"

"All you have to do is tell me exactly what you want, but there are rules. You can only wish for one item at a time, you can't wish someone back from the dead, and you can only wish for something to change in your own backyard. You can't wish that historic events never took place."

"What if my world affects the greater world? Doesn't it?"

"Yes, but you see, everyone's been following these rules with their genies for thousands of years. So, we are already part of the greater world. We already affect world events. Your wish may, in some ways we can't foresee, affect the outcome of some lives, and then others' lives, in a domino effect, but you can't specifically wish for historic events to never take place. Got it?"

"I think so. I have to wish for specific items relating to my personal life."

"That's right." He takes my hands in his. "Are you ready?"

"As ready as I'll ever be." I inhale deeply, then shout out: "I want to be thin in time for my high school reunion!"

"*Your wish is my command!*"

Purple smoke swirls around Eugene, who, seems

to have become a cyclone, madly circling around and around my living room.

I'm so startled, I grab my chest, and nearly pee my pants. I didn't think the transformation would be that big of a deal.

I touch my body, and realize something's missing. About half of it! I start feeling around for my legs and feet, because I can't, in fact, see them in all this purple haze. Then I reach for my backside.

"Holy crap, I have no ass left!" I start laughing. "I'm ass-less!" I can't believe this! Wait until the kids see me like this. Wait until Cathy sees me like this!

———

THE PURPLE SMOKE is starting to thin out, so I can see Eugene now. He's sitting on the sofa, legs and arms crossed, just grinning at me, with an 'I told you so!' look on his adorable face.

"Yes okay, yes, I believe you. I believe you. Look at this body!" I feel so young and beautiful, and I haven't even checked myself out in a mirror yet.

"You look amazing," he grins. "You have two more wishes, but you can call me from the Wii any time by giving it a rub, like you did the first time."

"I gave it a whack."

"Oh, yes, I wouldn't do that. Just rub it. Anyway, I should get back there until you've decided on your next wish."

"What? Oh."

I stare at him a moment, and wonder what it might be like to be held by him. Just held in his arms. He's so tall and strong, but his hands, his eyes — they're gentle, and kind. He's a bit grumpy, but I would be too if I'd been stuck inside bottles, lamps, and Wiis for thousands of years. And he's totally dorky, but I love that he knows stuff. I'd like to spend more time with him, I suddenly realize, and I'm going to have to ask for that. I take a stab at it.

"I... I was hoping for your company at the reunion tomorrow. I could use a date."

"A date? I haven't had a date in…" he hesitates for quite a while. "Ever. You sure you want to deal with a clumsy farmer at a dance?"

"Are you kidding; they're the best dates." I laugh, wondering what the hell I'm doing. "I don't want you to have to return to that cold dark existence. Please. You can stay downstairs. You're welcome to."

Eugene nods. "I'd really like that. Thanks. In fact, to show my gratitude, I'm taking you dress shopping tomorrow. My treat."

"Your treat? You genies carry money?"

"I have some stashed away for a rainy day, yes. It's my 'in case I'm ever free' stash."

"And you'd spend it on me?"

"I think you're worth it." He smiles, turns, and walks toward the kitchen. "I'm starving! Any more of those cheesies?"

I CAN HEAR Eugene rummaging around the kitchen cupboards, but I don't get up. He can find his own snacks. I need to just sit here and contemplate what's happened.

I look down at my arms, legs, and torso. Holy hell. My clothes shrunk along with my body. This babe could walk a runway! Mind you, not wearing those ridiculous designer outfits no sane person would ever contemplate – a paisley and peacock feather briefcase? Seriously, designers! Plus, I'm not sickly thin; there are still some curves and meat to me. I look healthy and feel so much lighter. I have to check out the mirror in the front hallway. I need to see myself!

I stare at my reflection for a full five minutes, inspecting every inch of my body, lifting my shirt and lowering the front and sides of my pants a little to feel the smooth skin beneath.

There's no cellulite on my hips, bum, thighs, and if that isn't just the most adorable little tummy I've ever seen. I've always wanted to say something positive about myself like that!

If this is a dream, it's the best dream, ever.

I almost pick up my phone and text my sister, but I can't quite come up with the words I'd use to explain the situation to her:

> Help. You know Aladdin? I think he's
> come to stay at my house.

No.

> Cici? I went on this crazy one-day
> diet, and I'm thin and going to my high
> school reunion tomorrow!

None of these work. Never thought I wouldn't be able to text my own sister. What's odd is that I kind of want to keep this my little secret for now. Even fun-loving Gram could spoil it all for me. My sis and Gram are pragmatic, and Gram is so protective of my well-being. She would definitely send Eugene to the psych ward at the local hospital if she knew he was essentially telling me he could solve all my problems.

Maybe I should tell Cici the truth, though.

> Hey. Funny thing happened today. A
> genie jumped out of my Wii and now
> I'm kind of dating him!

No, the truth won't set me free in this case. Right away she'd think it was a joke and probably wouldn't text back.

I'm dating a genie. This is unreal. Yesterday I was an overweight single Mom, and now I'm on the adventure of a lifetime with a hot Greek guy who wants to take care of me, and take me dress shopping.

It sounds too good to be true. Maybe I shouldn't

have leapt and let him stay with us. Maybe the date
will go horribly wrong, and I won't be able to get him
out of my head, or our house.

"Heymph. Theesh is shenomenal shuff!" Eugene
returns with a large plastic bowl of potato salad. He's
leaning against the doorframe, shovelling it in his
mouth by the spoonful. "Youph make theesh?" his
eyes smile at me but his mouth is busy, overflowing
with potato mush as he shovels it in, spoonful after
spoonful.

I'm reminded of The Beast in the Disney film. He
may seem like The Beast, but I'm certainly not Belle.
She had way too much patience for that slob.

"No, Gram made it, and, that's gross. You could
have found your own bowl instead of putting all your
germs into my serving dish."

"Oh." He immediately stops eating, wipes his
mouth with his shirt, puts the bowl down on the floor,
and sits close to me on the sofa. "Sorry. I just haven't
had food in so long. I forgot where I was."

"Yeah, about that. How much do you know about
me? About where I live? I mean, how are you going to
help me if you're thousands of years old?"

He looks at me with a blank stare. Is he hurt?
"Katherine, I'm not old. It's all relative. Think of it as
wise."

"Was it really wise to eat like that in front of me?"

"Perhaps it wasn't wise so much as necessary." He
chuckles. "Can we drop this now? Don't you modern

women ever drop anything, or is it just nag nag nag, all day long?"

"Woah." I push away from him a little.

Eugene chuckles and inches a little closer to me. "I was kidding. Look. I want to get to know you better. Tell me more about you."

"Huh. You didn't get a Coles Notes version of my life before you popped out of my Wii?" I joke.

"No, sadly, I've been given very little information on you."

"Seems like a sad excuse for a job, with little benefits, and no salary. Why are you doing this again?" I laugh, and look up at him. He's not smiling.

"Because I have to. I'm stuck doing it until I help more people." He looks down at his lap, and falls silent for a few moments.

I know a lot about what it feels like to be stuck in a situation. Sometimes, escaping is no easy feat. It was years before I even thought about finding the courage to leave Jimmy, but I still couldn't summon enough to do it. There was always an excuse. Usually, I made excuses for his behaviour. I also thought I was partly to blame. He made me believe that I was a lousy wife, and a horrible mother, and that's why he was so angry at me all the time. Me. My fault.

"I was stuck in an abusive marriage for a long time," I say softly. I stare at my hands, clasped together in my lap. They're more wrinkly than I remember. I wonder if my mother's hands looked like this at the same age.

"I'm sorry," Eugene says. He hesitates, then adds, "And, I'm sorry I didn't know you then." Then he surprises me by taking my hand in his, putting our clenched hands on his thigh, and leaning his head against the back of the sofa. It feels right, so I go along with it. I lean back so we're slouching together in silence. After a few moments, we exhale at the same time.

It's not an uncomfortable silence. It's comfortable. Right. Which makes me very uncomfortable! I shouldn't be feeling this way about a virtual stranger! I'm going to get my heart broken again if I'm not careful.

I have to say something, anything, to break the silence, but when I look over at Eugene, I realize he has fallen fast asleep.

Oh, and he snores. Perfect.

7

I'M GETTING A GENIE'S BED READY.

This guy who was strange to me 12 hours ago is no longer a stranger. Life sends you stuff you think you're supposed to be afraid of, abhor, push away, but sometimes, if you listen to the signals, to how it truly makes you feel, you realize it's the very stuff you should welcome into your life: Welcome with a sign, and flowers on the table, and an open heart.

I'm starting to think Eugene is like that.

As I pull the bottom sheet as far down as I can on the right corner of the futon mattress, a sleepy Eugene yawns and joins me at the left corner, pulling harder. I tug a little harder. He tugs even harder. *This isn't working.*

"Haven't you made a bed before, or are you like most men?"

"Wow. Sexist much?" He starts to chuckle. "Now

that's something we'd behead women for, where I come from."

I plunk myself down on the carpet, bowled over by his words. "What? What? And you'd allow that?" I inhale to calm myself down, but I can feel the temperature rising in my cheeks.

Eugene sits on the carpet, too, and holds up his hand. "Woah, woah, I was trying to make a joke. I'd never let a woman be beheaded. Do you think I'm the kind of man who'd allow that, who'd allow any inequalities between the sexes, when I let your Gram practically beat me to a pulp, and I'm sitting here struggling to make a bed for the first time?"

He smiles at me and starts putting a pillowcase on his pillow. I can't be mad at him when he smiles like that. I get up to finish tucking in the second sheet, then throw the comforter on top.

"Although," he continues, "when I was a free man, in some lands women were treated far better than how I've witnessed them being treated over the last century. In what you call Ancient Egypt, women could end up becoming Pharaoh, not just Queen, but Pharaoh."

"Pharaoh would be a step up from fat-loser-cashier." I giggle, and add, "Oh! Thin-loser-cashier now! I forgot." I can't help looking at my legs in these jeans. My eyes see the skinny, but my brain is having problems believing it.

Eugene doesn't laugh. He looks concerned for me. Disappointed.

"I don't want to hear you talking about yourself like that." He stops what he's doing, looks at me, and says in a near whisper, "We can change it all, you know. All of it."

All of it? Really? Does he even know what he's talking about? Because he said we can't bring people back from the dead. That's the greatest part of 'all of it.'

Ben is dead. Little, innocent Logan is dead. I can lose all the weight in the world and wish 1,000 wishes, but Eugene said it, clear as day. My heart desires it more than anything in this world, but I can't wish them back from the dead.

"By the way," Eugene's voice brings me back to reality… if I can call this reality. "This is so nice. You asked if I'd never made a bed before." His voice falls softer, "Actually, I've never slept in a real bed before. On the farm, we had hammocks, and since I've been a genie living inside lamps and man-made machines, well, we don't actually sleep."

"You don't sleep?" I sit beside him again.

"No, we're kind of on stand-by. We're on pause a lot of the time in between wishes. This is one of the first times a Master has tried to, or even wanted to, converse with me."

"I don't want to converse with you. You've forced me." I chuckle. He smiles.

"Once, I was Master to a woman who went to a Nordic spa every few months. She told me about these floating pools, where they'd lie back in the Epsom salt water, and just float for an hour. I wish my stasis felt like that. I wish I felt like I were floating. I'd feel free. I could have dreams of my own."

"It's not like that? How does it feel, when you're not with a Master, granting their wishes?"

"It feels like I'm frozen. It's cold and dark and quiet. I feel like I'm in a cave, and I can't move."

"That's awful! How do you live like that?"

"I don't have a choice, Katherine. I don't have choices anymore. My Masters have the choice. I try to enjoy the times I'm out of stasis, like this, when I can make other people happy."

I study his face for a moment. His eyes look quite young, virtually wrinkle-free at the corners, but I know there must be thousands of years of pain hidden behind them. His jaw is square and strong, but I wonder if his strength ever waivers. This guy seems more trapped in his life than me! Does he ever let it all out and cry, like I do?

"So when was the last time you felt in control of your own life?" I decide to ask outright.

"Wow, Oprah, why don't you just cut to the chase," he puts a pillow behind him, leans back against the wall, and stretches his legs out on the carpet. I sit cross-legged, hugging the other pillow.

Neither of us wants to acknowledge the bed is there, or that we could sit together on it.

Eugene looks at me, but says nothing for a whole minute. It reminds me of a how a cat looks at a new object, quizzically at first, not even touching it, just sitting still and staring it down to see if it's an object it should trust. I keep staring back at him until I'm too uncomfortable, and then I look away at a spot on the carpet. To my surprise, he breaks the silence with an answer.

"I guess I felt in control of my family life. Things were going pretty well for us before..." he looks away.

"You were a farmer before all this started, right?" I hesitate. "Did you have a wife? A family?"

He looks down at his lap and sighs.

"I thought this – all of this – was about you."

"No, it's about you, too, since it appears we're in this together."

"I was married. Yes. She died a few days after giving birth, from an infection," he almost whispers.

"Oh, I'm sorry." I don't know what to say now. I think about his child, or children, and want to ask what's happened to them, if he'll ever see them again, in his own time, but I can see by the look on his face that he won't be able to handle talking about it. After a while, he finally speaks.

"I have a nine-year-old son," he pauses a moment. "Had, I suppose." His voice cracks. "I haven't seen him since I was cursed. If I can break the curse,

everything in my time goes back exactly as it was —
but I can't seem to break it."

"God," I say. I look at him for a long time.

"And even if I break the curse, I can get back to
my son, but my wife… she's gone. I can't get her
back."

I want to move toward him and hug him, but I'm
not sure he'll know it's authentic; and I'm not sure he
wants a pity party. "I'm sorry," I say again, suddenly
feeling the weight of his world.

"I wish I could freeze time," he says. "I can time
travel, though not especially well, but I haven't
learned how to freeze moments in time. That would
be…" he pauses, searching for the right word,
"astounding."

"Oh, yeah, that would take my breath away," I
agree. I wonder what moment I'd choose to freeze.

As if reading my mind, Eugene asks me the very
same question. There's a hint of a smile on his face
again as he asks. I'd better answer. This discussion is
lifting that dismal mood we'd created before. But first,
I need to know something.

"I'm not sure yet. You brought it up. You must
know what you'd want to freeze in time?"

"The day my son was born. The look on my wife's
face as I handed him to her. That. I'd freeze that in
time." His voice is unwavering. I can tell he's thought
about that moment many times.

I wonder what his wife was like. I feel a lump

forming in my throat, but swallow it down, then clear my throat. I don't want him to see all of me yet. "The birth of my girls were life-changing moments, but I think I'd pick a time when I was in a little less pain."

Eugene smirks.

"Maybe a summer vacation?"

"We never had those as a family. We couldn't. Jimmy couldn't be trusted. I tried to keep him away from my daughters as much as possible. Still do." I wipe the spot under my nose with my sleeve. Damn. It's running, and my throat is tight. I'm going to cry any minute if I'm not careful.

Oh, let it go, Cat. Let it go. He's told you about losing his wife, and how he hasn't seen his son in years. He's opening up. You should try it, too. Open your heart. Let him in.

One deep inhale, another look in his eyes, and I proceed, with caution at first. "I hate what I put those girls through. I hate myself for making so many mistakes in my past that meant my girls couldn't even enjoy a regular childhood."

"You need to forgive yourself, Katherine. Let it go, and move forward."

"Uh, we really are on the Oprah show aren't we, Dr. Phil?"

"Come on, you know what I mean. It's a heavy load to haul. Unhitch the trailer."

"Unhitch the trailer. I like that. I love that, in fact. There's another one I made up, too."

"Try it on me."

"If life is a highway, I'm done being stuck behind the manure truck."

Eugene chuckles. "Perfect. I can help you with that. Back to your moment. What would you freeze?"

"I guess it would be the one vacation we did manage to take, without Jimmy. After the divorce. I have this teal blue Mason jar I love, with a little glass lid on it. I found it for five dollars at a flea market. I hid it at the back of our closet, under some clothes he thought I was planning on mending, and started stuffing cash in there when the abuse started. I thought of it as my Exit Fund, and that helped me survive each new day. I never could find the courage to leave him, but that jar – that jar of cash – kept me going."

"Where'd you get the cash?"

"Oh, change from here and there that he'd leave on the kitchen table. He'd empty his pockets after work. I just took what I thought he wouldn't miss."

Eugene nods, then stands up, stretches, and lets out a yawn. To my surprise, he takes his pillow, then takes mine from my hand, fluffs them up a little, and tosses them against the wall, which is acting as the futon's headboard. He sits down, stretches out his legs, relaxes his back into the pillow, and pats the place beside him.

"Come on. It's more comfy up here. I won't bite."

"I know you won't," I sit next to him. "You didn't

even get my 'Fifty Shades' reference, I doubt you're into Vampires either."

He doesn't blink. I think I'm going to have to get him to spend a little time on Google.

"So, where did you take your girls with that money?"

"Well, it was enough for gas money, and food, but not for a hotel, so we had one beautiful, long day in Maine, and a lot of driving and sleeping in the car. But it was perfection."

———————

I CAN STILL FEEL the warm wind on my face from the top of that Ferris wheel. It caressed my face like the sun. The sky was celestial blue, not a cloud to be seen; the ocean below, a mirror image of the sky, and the beach, a long stretch of pristine white sand.

A silly grin spread across my face, and not just because of the stunning view. My girls were seated opposite me, saying, "Wow! Cool!" every 30 seconds. They were pointing at people below, tiny ants on the sand, and giggling because the ride had suddenly stopped.

"We get to stay up here a while? This is incredible!" Jenna said. She was watching a boat pull a parasailor behind it.

Alyssa was chewing pink bubble gum. Her eyes grew wide as she looked at the town on one side of the Ferris wheel, then moved to the other side to look at the parasailor with Jenna. Her bubble kept getting bigger, but it didn't pop. That's how I felt. Like my love for my girls had grown stronger than I ever thought possible, and that my heart might burst from happiness.

Jenna popped Alyssa's bubble, and the two laughed it off. I love it when they're getting along. They had also been sharing more secrets with me. I heard about the boy Alyssa got texts from, and the career Jenna was interested in, and was able to give advice without once being told to mind my own business.

The wind had set my hair into a mess of wild strands, but I didn't care. Laughing, I took one loose strand that had gotten caught in my mouth, and swept it off my face. I loved how my skin smelled like coconut scented sunscreen, and my hair tasted like the salty ocean.

As we watched the parasailor fade into the horizon, Jenna looked over at me and took my hand. "Thanks for this trip, Mom. I'll never forget it."

"THAT WAS MY MOMENT," I tell Euguene. "I wish I could freeze that time, on top of the world."

Eugene smiles. He looks relaxed. "It would be a powerful tool, being able to stop time, wouldn't it?" he asks, stretching his arms out. His hand brushes my shoulder by accident. I can't believe how much that matters. I feel like a teenage girl around him!

"Yes, but I'll settle for three wishes. I think that's enough excitement for one week," I laugh. I could stay up all night talking with him, but I'd better leave this bed now. I stand up and stretch, feigning that I'm tired.

"Goodnight. Let me know if there's anything else you need."

"Thanks for your hospitality, you and your grandmother, Her Royal Badass."

"Yes, well let's hope she doesn't come downstairs, forget you're here by invitation, and attack you in the middle of the night."

"I can only hope. And prepare the moves I learned from an old Samurai." He slides under the covers now that I'm off the bed, then pulls the blankets up to his chin as I turn out the light.

"Katherine? I never knew beds were so comfy. I kind of hope you take your time coming up with your wishes."

I smile because I have a new friend, and I needed one. I smile, knowing he can't see it in the darkness.

"Goodnight, Eugene."

Once upstairs, I undress, and twirl around with my new body, staring at myself in my bedroom mirror for a good five minutes. I'm not sorry I'm having a few moments of vanity – I need to make up for lost time.

I open up my top dresser drawer. What am I going to wear to bed now that I'm so many pounds lighter?

To my surprise, there are several new nighties and nightshirts in the drawer. All the right size for my new body. I check the second drawer: t-shirts, jeans, socks and... the third drawer down: oh my, lacy underwear! How'd he know my preference? And the nighties are silk. *Who knew a guy named Eugene could have such good taste?*

I notice there's a sticky note placed on top of some of the shirts:

> *You deserve this little extra. Consider this new wardrobe and the dress we'll buy tomorrow a gift. You still have two wishes left. Thanks for having me stay with you. ~Eugenius*

I pull on the teal blue coloured silk negligee, with gorgeous lace insets at the sides, and turn in a circle, checking out my reflection from every angle. *Nice.* I actually like the image in the mirror for the first time in over twenty years.

I turn off the light and crawl into bed, but it's

hard to turn off my mind. So much has happened today. What will tomorrow bring? What else should I wish for? I wish Eugene were a real man. Well, he says he's a real man, and his body sure looks real. As in, real good! *But he lives in a Wii, Cat. I don't think he's an option.*

I chuckle out loud.

Calm your mind, Cat. Go to sleep, now. You have to stop thinking of him that way. He is not an option.

Eugene reminds me a little of Ben. Ben loved to surprise me, too. He used to say, "It's the little things that can make all the difference." I remember our prom night, how he presented me with a friendship bracelet he'd made, and showed me how it matched one he'd made for himself. I wore it for years, until it finally fell off, and I lost it.

PROM WAS SUCH A BEAUTIFUL NIGHT. A light summer's breeze. A clear sky covered with a soft blanket of stars. Ben had presented me with the red bracelet, which matched my dress, and a white lily for my hair.

We went to the ceremony together, but after a while, we ditched the dance. Ben saw everyone staring at me, making fun of me on the dance floor, and told me he wanted it all to stop, all the pain and heartache, at least for one night.

"Cat?" Ben's mouth whispered in my ear. I could

feel him blowing in it, but it wasn't an attempt to turn me on. It was to get the long strands of hair out of the way so they'd stop ending up in his mouth.

"Yeah," I giggled. That tickled.

"Let's get out of here," he said, and he took my hand and led me to the parking lot to his new, but of course used, 1976 white Mustang Cobra. Letting go of my hand, he tapped the top of the Mustang, which was painted with a thick black racing stripe.

"She's a beauty," I said. "I'm glad I was able to lend you some money so you could have it in time for graduation." Ben had wanted this car for months, but had lost his job at the grocery store when it temporarily closed for expansion. It was going to reopen in July, and he was hoping to pull in 40 hours per week. When I offered part of my college fund, he assured me he would pay back every penny I'd taken from the fund within two months of working again. That way, I'd still have my tuition covered for September.

"Thank you, Cat. I'll never forget it." I looked up – way up, he was six feet tall, and I was only five foot one – at his almond coloured eyes and jet-black hair. Such a contrast. Kind of like him and me. We were so different, and yet, so similar in everything that mattered.

"Don't worry about it. The money was just sitting there in my savings, and I know you'll pay me back in time for school." I hoped he'd take my hand again soon. It was chilly outside. He noticed me shivering, opened the car door to grab his school jacket, and placed it gently over my shoulders. Then he turned me around to face him, and turned my chin upward, cupping it gently in his hand like precious drinking water.

"I'm so proud of you for getting into business college," he said, and with his other arm, he gave me a squeeze. You're going to be the best bookstore manager this town has ever seen. And maybe I'll get out of groceries and come work for you." He chuckled.

"I'm a bitch to work for," I said. "I don't give extra breaks, and you definitely can't make out with your coworkers, or heaven forbid, your manager, when you're at work."

Ben laughed. "Well I guess I'm going to have to get as much of that as I can in now then." His soft lips brushed mine, gently at first, then, full of passion.

We'd kissed many times before that school year, but this kiss was different. It said he was proud of me. It said he didn't see the fat. He saw me. It said we were going to make it through the summer and adapt to me being in college while he was working. It said we were forever, and I didn't want it to end.

"Cat," Ben slowly stopped our kiss, but as he drew away, he kept looking me in the eyes. "I want to take you to Murphy's point," he whispered, "but it's just to relax and look at the stars, okay? You don't have to do anything you don't want to..." He took a wisp of curly hair that had fallen in front of my eyes and tucked it behind my ear.

I remember looking in his eyes, and feeling that he meant it. "It's okay, I know that, and I'd like to go."

Everyone in our town knew what Murphy's point was for, so much so that there were cops patrolling the area pretty much 24/7, and making out with cop cars nearby was far from romantic. But I didn't want to go all the way, even in a romantic environment, and Ben knew that, and respected it. It was something we'd talked about a lot. We'd known each other a long time, but we'd only being going out a couple months. We were going to take our time.

I wish I'd known then that time wasn't on our side. I wish I'd known that night, that long lovely night when he let me sleep in his arms on a blanket under the stars, that it would be our last night together.

8

THE NEXT MORNING, BEN woke me with a kiss on
each eyelid. I smiled, stretched, and sat up, looking
around. The grass was freshly covered in dew, the sun
was shining; the day felt full of promise.

"Hi," I smiled, and kissed his lips. "Last night was
wonderful. Thank you."

He barely had a chance to say: "You're welcome,"
before my panic set in.

"Oh God, we stayed here all night? My Gram!
Gram! She's going to be worried sick about me!"
Gram was my family. My only family.

My parents had died in a car accident when I was
three years old. I barely remembered them. It wasn't
like I could miss what I'd never had, so when people
pitied me over it, I just shrugged my shoulders and
said, "Hey, it's life. You can go with it, or fight against
it. I choose to make the most of what I've got." I

didn't really feel that way – I did sometimes wish I had my parents to take me to Disneyland and do things with me and Cici that Gram felt too old to do. But all in all, she was a great friend and confidante. She taught me about my period, and sex, and drugs, and her version of rock and roll (she was one of the few of her generation who liked Elvis the Pelvis), and never minced words. She was frank, and helpful, and fair. We'd weathered a lot of storms together, and come out better for them.

Ben put his hands on my shoulders to try to calm me down. "Cat, take a breath. I went to the Tourism Centre over there late last night and called her up. I told her we came here after the dance and said we wanted to camp out. It's fine."

"You've got to be kidding me. She didn't freak out?"

"She was your unique and loving Gram. You know she isn't that strict. She gets you."

"Yes, she does." I sighed and relaxed back onto our blanket.

"In fact, she sounded more concerned about the bears than she did me. She warned me there'd been a bear attack a couple weeks ago. Not here, of course."

I laughed. "Oh, I'm surprised she didn't mail you a newspaper clipping about it." Gram's clippings were infamous in our household. She'd clip articles she felt I should pay attention to, and pinned them to the bulletin board on my bedroom door. When I was at a summer mini-university course a few years before, she actually mailed clippings, ones about Drive-by shootings and that drug people put in your drink, to my dorm room. Daily.

"It's okay, she had one there and read the entire article to me over the phone." We laughed together until my sides hurt. I think, in that moment, I loved Ben and my Gram a little more than I had the day before. If that was at all possible.

The sound of screeching car tires interrupted our blissful silence. Someone was revving their car in the parking lot behind us, where Ben had parked his car. Ben stood up and covered his eyes from the sun with his hand, like a visor, so he could see what was going on over there. "It's Jake. Jake's here in his Mustang, Cat."

If Cathy Hollows was my least favourite person at Trudeau High, Jake Hampton was Ben's. Jake had had it in for Ben from the moment he'd stood up for me at that pool party. It didn't take long before Ben had heard enough of the teasing. He had taken a strawberry banana smoothie that was out on a patio table, and dumped it over Jake's head. In front of all their friends. Jake tried to punch Ben in retaliation, but Ben ducked, and instead, Jake punched Jimmy. I had stood back and laughed as the scene developed into more physical comedy than even the Three Stooges could pull off. Before they knew what hit them, both Jake and Jimmy were lying on the grass with bloody noses, Angie, Cathy and all their classmates were laughing at them, and Ben had grabbed a plateful of snacks from Jake's fridge and headed out the front door, with me by his side. I'd been by his side pretty much every day since.

"Hey losers!" Jake stood up on the seat of his car, leaned over his windshield, and gave us the finger. "We been lookin' for ya." Some of his buddies were in the back, snickering.

Ben clenched his left fist, and walked right up to Jake's car. "What do you want, Jake. School's over. What do you want?"

"Your car, dipshit. I want your car. I'd like a pair of Stangs in my driveway, and your face plastered on the pavement on that stretch of road over there." He motioned to the winding stretch of country road that led to Murphy's point. It was treacherous to speed on it, and it barely had space for two cars racing side-by-side, but time and word of mouth had made it the popular place for teenage boys to race their cars. Two teens had been killed there in the last decade, but that wasn't about to stop Jake. Nothing would stop Jake when he was out for revenge.

"You wanna race?" Ben showed no fear. "I'm in."

"Ben! Stop it! You don't need to do this," I called out from inside Ben's car. I'd felt too vulnerable standing there, so I'd packed up our blanket and hidden away inside the car.

Ben turned around and talked to me through the

windshield. "Yes, Cat, I do. This has to stop. Let's put it to rest." He turned back to Jake and his followers. "Okay, let's do it tonight. As soon as it gets dark. Meet you here."

Jake and his friends seemed satisfied. They started hooting and hollering, throwing beer cans out of the car. Jake started his Mustang, revved its engine, and sped off. Ben stood there in the dust a few moments by himself. He just stood there. Then he walked to his car and got in.

I couldn't breathe. I wanted to vomit, but I said and did nothing. God, I wish I'd said more to stop it all from unravelling, but I just let him drive me home.

I said and did nothing.

THE DRIVE UP to the flat stretch before Murphy's point that evening was eerily silent. Usually, Ben put music on while we were driving, but he turned the radio off twice when I tried to improve the atmosphere with some tunes. Except for a, "Hey," he was lost in his own thoughts from the moment he picked me up at Gram's, just after 6 p.m., until I broke the silence ten minutes later.

"Ben."

He kept his eyes on the road.

"Ben. You don't have to do this."

"I want to do this. I need to show that guy he's not King Shit of this town."

"And drag racing him proves what? That you are? Or maybe they'll crown you Stupid Shit."

"Did you really just call me that?" he clenched the steering wheel harder, his knuckles turning white. The anger in his tone surprised me. "I'd expect that from my father, Cat, but not from you. Never from you." His voice was softer. Hurt.

"Stop the car, Ben. I see them up ahead, but I need a moment alone with you. Please."

"Fine." Ben pulled his Mustang over to the side of the dirt road, hard and fast, kicking up clouds of grey dust that enveloped the car. In the moments before it settled, he turned off the engine, and we just sat there, staring out through the glass to the outside world. It felt like we were caught up inside the eye of a tornado. Deceptively safe inside the car; grave danger looming outside.

I touched his arm, and he turned to look at me, frowning. "Ben, is that what this is about? Your father? I know he gives you a hard time, but how is this going to change anything?"

Ben took a deep breath, and for a second, I wondered if he was choking back tears. It looked like it, but then he looked down, so I couldn't see his eyes. "He says I don't stand up for myself enough. He was so disappointed when I didn't make the football team. He actually called me a wimp the other day."

I knew Ben's father was especially tough on him, his only son, but I didn't realize he'd picked on him like this. I just wanted to reach out and hug him.

"I just can't let Jake win this time. He's done this kind of thing to me since Kindergarten, and on top of that, Dad's friends with Jake's parents. Dad always mentions how athletic Jake is. He even told me I should ask Jake how he trained for football tryouts. As if! If he only knew!"

"But you should tell him. Tell him how he bullies you."

He turned, sighed, and took my chin in his hand. "Sweetheart, I can't go running to Daddy every time someone upsets me. I'm going to be living on my own soon. Besides, I don't want to be the butt of everyone's jokes this summer. Jake, Jimmy, Angie, Cathy... they're going to be watching what happens here. If I don't race, they'll probably never invite me to any of their parties again. I'll become uncool in their eyes." He let his hand drop, and stared at his lap. He couldn't look at me.

"Again? Since when did you go to any of their parties, except when we were kids? What are you even talking about?" I couldn't believe he'd brought up Cathy Hollows in conversation. He knew she'd been horrible to me all through high school. What was he doing even thinking about her?

"You don't get it, sweetie. You're getting out of

town soon. Going off to college, hours away. But not me. I'm stuck here. With them."

"You can't stand Jake. Why would you want to hang out with him... ever?"

"I don't think I have a choice here, Cat. I need to make him respect me, and then I'll have a chance fitting in with his crowd. See, Dad tells me that..."

"Holy shit, Ben, you're actually listening to your father? He doesn't know what he's talking about! Your father's only friends with Jake's Dad because they do business together!" Jake's Dad owned a successful car dealership in town, and Ben's father is his lawyer. "It's a business relationship, Ben. I wouldn't call it a friendship."

"Well, whatever, I'm going to need friends when you're away." He kept staring at the steering wheel.

"Ben! I'm not leaving you when I go off to college. We'll be in touch, every day."

"I know, and I'm not leaving you. I just... things are going to be different. I'm going to be different. It's time I took a stand." With that, he kissed me quickly on the lips, turned his key in the ignition, and began revving the engine.

"You have to get out now," he said, lowering his head, and his voice. I could hear the fear in it, but he wouldn't look at me. He wouldn't let me see his face.

I sat there in complete shock. Whatever conversation he'd had with his father; whatever party he'd attended at Jake's parents' place that I didn't know about; whatever had happened to make him want Jimmy, Angie, and Cathy on his side, I suddenly realized that I wasn't privy to that information. In that moment, I realized I didn't know him at all like I thought I did. It took a few more decades for it all to sink in.

I didn't know what to say, or what to do, so I said and did nothing. I opened the car door, got out, but stuck my head in to say goodbye. "I love you, Ben Coverdrive. You come back to me in one piece. Please."

He smiled, but kept staring straight ahead. "Don't worry. I'll be fine."

I could hear Jake's car coming up behind me, fast, so I quickly stepped behind the Mustang, onto the side of the road near a ditch. I was wearing flip flops, overalls, a white t-shirt, and a black cardigan, and when I looked down, I noticed my feet were already covered in dust. They looked almost dark-skinned. Feeling a chill across my back, I pulled my cardigan tighter across my chest, giving myself a hug. It was dusk now, and dozens of cars were lining up behind us to watch the big event. I guess we'd inadvertently created the starting line I didn't want to exist.

Jake pulled up alongside Ben, gave us an inane toothy grin, then pulled a quick U-turn so the front of his car was pointed in the same direction as the Mustang: North toward Murphy's point. He was alone in his car, but he was waving and giving a "thumbs up" to a carload of people behind him. It was hard to make out who everyone was, but I could definitely see Cathy's profile. I noticed Ben looking back at them over his shoulder, too.

Then she got out of the car. She made a point of looking my way, but didn't smile. She walked up to Jake's car, giving her ass an all too obvious extra wiggle, and bent down to whisper in his ear. As they conversed, she stuck out her bum, jean shorts riding up, up and away. It was clear to me she was doing this for Ben, because she looked his way several times and smiled. How had I not noticed her attraction to him before this? Where had I been?

But Ben wasn't looking at Cathy's ass cheeks. When I glanced back in his direction, I saw him looking at me. He was smiling, that smile I adored, but there was something new behind it. Fear. I'd never seen him look so scared. I almost stepped forward and stood in front of his car. Almost. But Cathy broke the silence.

"Okay, people." She walked to the space between Ben's and Jake's cars and pulled out a small plastic Canadian flag from her inside jean-jacket pocket. "Let's have a race to remember! Jake said I can call it. When this flag goes down, hit the gas, boys! And may the best man win!" She put one hand on her hip, and raised her other hand with the flag high in the air, giggling.

Was this all a big joke to her?

There are parts of that night that remain locked inside my memory vault, never to escape. Maybe that's good. Maybe not. I've lived with vague memories and half memories of that night for half my life, but the part that happened next? I haven't forgotten one minute. Not one second. It's a deep dark scar in my memory, and it never fades.

The red and white flag went down. I jumped backward into the ditch, trying to avoid the dust and pebbles that were kicked up almost immediately by eight spinning tires. Engines revving, hearts pounding, men shouting, someone whistling. I looked behind me and saw hundreds of people I knew from school, acquaintances, standing on their parked cars, hooting and hollering, fists in the air. Jimmy Fink, crushing a beer can with one hand. Cathy Hollows, standing on the hood of her own car, still waving the flag. More hollering, and sparklers? Yes, someone had lit sparklers. It was starting to spit rain. Cold, dark, rain. *Weeeaaaaaaaaa.* A siren. That was a police siren. *Thank God. They'll stop it. They'll stop this in time.*

I couldn't bear to look ahead up the road, to the racing cars, but I did. And when I did, I saw Jake's car sideswiping Ben's. The Mustang swerved, and its back end nearly ended up in the ditch, but the race continued. Jake was in the lead. *Where was that police car?* I turned my head to look. *The police car is behind all the parked cars. It can't get past.*

Someone's coming up beside me in a small green car. Jimmy

Fink. He winked at me. Cathy, Angie, and another girl I didn't know were squished in the backseat. There was a trophy on the front seat. I jumped in fast, despising myself, but knowing it was the only way to reach the finish line right after they crossed and avoid the riot scene behind us, where some of our rowdy peers were being arrested.

I threw the trophy down at my feet, but not before noticing the engraved name and date. Murphy's Point '93: WINNER Jake Hampton. It was already engraved! Those disgusting egos. I wanted to vomit. I looked up and saw we were catching up to Ben and Jake. Closer, closer. I peered around their cars and saw the winding stretch of road in front of them. We were nearly at the top of the point.

Oh God. No. No!

A big black dog was in front of Ben's car, to the left side of the road, but right in Ben's path. He would swerve. *Come on Ben, miss it! Miss it!*

Ben slammed on his brakes, and I heard the sound of breaking glass. Jake kept driving forward. Jimmy slammed on his brakes, hard, and I was out of the car and running before he even stopped it. I don't know how. Adrenaline fueled my breath, and I ran faster than I've ever run before; faster than any track meet I'd ever trained for, but it was too late. Seconds too late.

A small white shoe sailed across the air slowly, like

a parachute. I ran toward it, but it flew up and away from in front of Ben's car to the left side of the road.

Parachutes are bright and beautiful. This shoe was covered in blood.

The black dog was beside the shoe now, lying in the ditch, wailing. Sirens wailing, dog wailing, small bloodied child lying on the road, not making a sound. Not one sound.

On my knees, my hands covering the child's tiny chest, but all this blood, flowing onto the road like a river. Blood soaked boy, blue lips, Oh God where is Ben? Ben help me! Help me!

Large strong hands pulled me up and away from the dying child. I turned to face my Ben. But it wasn't Ben. It was a stranger in a uniform. I started shaking. "Where's Ben? He'll help. He knows CPR. Where's Ben?" I heard my frightened screams echoing in the darkness but sat alone in the ditch, waiting for Ben to make everything bright again. He never came.

I STOOD by Ben's bed in Emergency, held his hand, and watched him die. I intuitively knew I was watching him die. I'd been told that his body had been flung through the car's front windshield. But I kept thinking it was a waking dream. It couldn't be real.

Ben was breathing rapidly for quite some time. I felt a sense of hope rise up inside me. Then, he ceased breathing. A few moments later, a sharp intake of breath again. I felt the hope rise again, but then his breathing ceased completely, and his body began to quiver.

Beep. Beep. Beep. Beeeeeeeeeeeeeep.

Suddenly, a hush came over the room. An eerie hush, followed by the sound of hustling and bustling around me. I heard someone mutter, "Should she be here?" and someone else reply, more quietly, "Shh, she's the fiancée." I felt like I was in a trance from the moment the officer pulled me away from the little boy's body to the time he put me in a car behind the ambulances, but I'd had enough common sense to lie to the nurses when I came in. I told them I was his fiancée, and they rushed me to the Emergency Room. I didn't see his father or mother. I was the first one there. The only one who watched Ben die.

"Time of death, seven-ten."

I heard it, but it didn't compute. I kept talking to Ben like he was still alive.

"Sweetheart, you can pull through," I said, bending down to kiss his cheek and lips. I heard fast footsteps, authoritative voices, machinery being unplugged behind me, but no one was asking me to move, so I didn't.

I stood there for what seemed like forever, caressing his cheek, but then it started to feel cold, and suddenly, he gasped for air. I stopped caressing him and, panic-stricken, called out for help.

"Someone! Anyone! He's trying to breathe! Help him! Please help him!"

A short, dark-haired nurse came over and gently pulled me away from Ben's ceasing body. "Oh, love, I'm so sorry, so so sorry," she said. "He's not with us anymore."

I couldn't hear or see anything. Everything started turning dark, and I lost my balance. She guided me to a chair in the waiting room, and sat me down. I guess she thought it was the best place for me, but what I heard next would haunt my dreams.

"*No!* Logan! Nooo!" The ear-piercing scream came from the Emergency entrance. A woman in her forties ran through the glass doors, her coat unbuttoned. She was wearing pajama bottoms and a t shirt. A police officer was not far behind her. A very young blond-haired doctor raced to her side and took her elbow, escorting her away from the operating rooms, where she'd been headed. He tried to push her gently to where I was seated, but she hit him on the shoulder with her purse, and began pounding his chest.

"He's dead isn't he?"

The doctor could only nod and look down at his feet.

The woman wailed and pounded his chest again. "My innocent boy, my boy! Why couldn't you save him? Why? Why?" she gasped for air, but kept sobbing and screaming out Logan's name.

The doctor stood there with an expressionless face and just took it until the officer gently parted their two shaking bodies, and tried to console the grief stricken woman, who crumpled like a rag doll in his arms. I started shaking and crying myself, and when I looked a little closer, I saw the young doctor had tears in his eyes, but he wasn't going to let them fall in front of anyone. He walked away quickly, and the officer escorted the woman to another area of the hospital. It suddenly got strangely silent around me. Everyone in Emergency was dealing with the remains of this accident, and I was left alone on a hard, cold chair, in a room that reeked of sickness and Savlon, wondering what, if anything, remained for me.

I don't know how long I sat there until Gram came for me and took me home. I also don't know how long it took… months…? Years…? before I could visit a hospital again, but I was forced to do so when Jenna was born. That was a joyful day, despite her father choosing not to be present. Joyful, and yet I remember after they handed me my baby, wrapped in a pink blanket, the first thing I did was put my ear to her lips, to assure myself that she was breathing.

I stood by both my girls' cribs and beds, checking to be sure they were never gasping for air like Ben, every single night of their young lives, until they were old enough to tell me to go away.

9

Sun streams in from my bedroom's far window and caresses my face, waking me gently with its warmth and light. As I sit up in bed and stretch my arms above my head, I notice something different. They aren't like weights. They feel as light as wings! *I've got wings! I've got wings!*

Ok, Cat, enough. You're starting to sound like an Always *commercial.*

I jump out of bed and face the floor-length mirror.

God, the nightmares last night. I hate remembering. Every single night. Why do I have to remember, every single night of my life? I have to push the memories aside. I have to. I'm alive, I'm thin, and I'm going to my reunion tonight!

I shall push the bad feelings *out*, and allow the good feelings to flow back *in*. I am a Yoga Master,

Master of the Breath, Master of the *Zen* in a world of chaos.

I look at myself in the mirror again, raise my arms above my head in a sun salutation, and pretend to be a badass yoga instructor:

"*People! People!* Don't let the moves sacrifice your *breath!*"

I giggle out loud now but continue bending down, pushing my head in between my legs, and placing my hands flat on the floor. *Wow. Wow! I'm fit enough now to do this yoga crap and actually look like I know what I'm doing! I gotta try more.*

I've always wanted to try the bridge pose. It looks like the best back stretch in the world.

Okay, let's see. I lie down on the floor on my back, stretch out my legs, and place the soles of my feet flat on the floor. I raise my hips, then push my hands behind my head, placing my palms on the floor, and away from me. I push up on those hands as hard as I can. I can see my hips and pelvis rising slowly. My head is falling backward. Up. Up. Up. Up. I'm upside down. Oh *my* God …this feels…so… *wrong* Just *wrong!*

Ahhhhhhhhhhhhhhhhh!

In about three seconds, I am quite certain I shall collapse on this floor, breaking my back in the process.

Help! Help! Somebody, a little help here!

Creeeeak. My door opens.

A pair of green eyes is staring right into mine. I try to smile at Eugene, but of course, it comes off as an upside down smile, which looks like a frown. Especially since I'm clenching my teeth and trying not to swear.

"*Why did I put myself in this position? Fuckity! Fuckity!*"

I'd started saying *Fuckity* when Jenna was in preschool, in a pathetic attempt to fool her that Mommy wasn't actually swearing, but reciting a word from a nursery rhyme. It hadn't conned either of my kids, not for a minute, and while they grew up, the word I'd concocted stuck with me. I love how it flies from my lips, a word-dart of frustration, sailing into the air with far more grace and humour than *Fuck* ever could. *Fuckity*.

"Is that some kind of wish? You should be more clear." Eugene smirks, and I almost laugh. But it hurts to laugh.

"*Eugene*. Get me out of this position. Please!"

He stifles his laughter, puts one of those giant gentle hands at my lower back, and another one at my head, and slowly pushes me up, so I'm halfway standing. I shake my legs and arms and tilt my head forward and to either side, hoping it will feel like it's on my shoulders again soon.

"Yeah, about this," Eugene says. "You may be thin now, but even thin people need to work their way up slowly to more challenging workouts."

"Sure, thanks for the tip." I groan and grab the hand towel on my dresser to wipe the sweat from my forehead.

As I bury my face in the towel, I can see through the fibres and notice Eugene is staring at me. Not like a robot would. Like a man would. Oh. I'd forgotten I was wearing that teal negligee. It's cut three inches above the knees. I figure he must be a thigh man, because that's where he's looking.

I haven't had a man look at me like this in years. Jimmy stopped looking as soon as I gave birth to Jenna. He even told me I wasn't attractive because my breasts were full of milk. "You're like a cow." By then, I was getting used to the derogatory comments, but I still wasn't brave enough to kick him out. I got pregnant with Alyssa a year and a bit later, one drunken night at the foot of the bed. Jimmy came in after last call at the bar around the corner, and told me exactly what he wanted, and not politely either. I could tell he was beyond drunk, and I didn't want my face cut up again, so I chose the lesser of two evils. I don't think he even kissed me.

I bury my face further into the towel, hoping the moment will just pass. It doesn't. He's still staring at my legs. I feel light and beautiful, and find myself smiling into the towel. *Thank you, Eugene.*

I throw the towel on the bed and look at him. Not wanting to be caught in the act, his eyes dart up to meet mine. He picks up the towel and throws it toward the hamper across the room. He doesn't miss. *Impressive!*

"So, where are you taking me shopping today,

Master? Oh. Do me a favour? No antique stores, okay? I've seen enough old lamps to last me a lifetime, or three." His abrupt change of subject and body language is far from smooth, but I go along with it.

"These aren't wishes, right?" I ask. "I don't want to use up a wish accidentally."

"No, Katherine. If you want to make one of your next two wishes, you have to look me in the eyes and hold my hands like last time. I'm not going to punk you out of a wish. I just think you deserve a nice dress. So, we shall find you one." He walks toward the door, opens it farther, then stands there for a moment on the other side, looking at my legs again.

"I have one request, though. Can you change out of that negligee? Please?" He grins.

"Yeah, yeah," I say, "I'll just put on one of my many Chitons, made of fine, long, pleated linen, so I look more like those Greek chicks you're used to." I chuckle and start to shut the door.

"Doric Chiton or Ionic Chiton?" he calls from the gap that's still left. "There's a difference, you know. The Doric is longer at the overfold. And… you don't have to cover up that much," he adds from behind the now-closed-door.

"Whatever!" I laugh. "Meet you outside." Everything feels so good. So easy. Maybe too easy. *Snap out of this, Cat. You need to remember you can't trust any man with your heart. Ever.*

I PARK the car in front of Walmart and take the keys out of the ignition.

"Okay, here we are, let's go." He's still sitting there.

"Walmart? For a high school reunion dress? Seriously, Katherine?" He shakes his head.

"What? I thought it wasn't a bad idea."

"It's not a great idea, either. You want to wow people you haven't seen in a while, you get a dress no one else has seen, or will show up in."

"Oh. How do you know all this?"

"I served the Kardashians, remember? They had everything custom-designed for them when I was their Master."

"But we don't have time for that. I need a dress for tonight!" I feel panic setting in. Suddenly, I realize I care about my appearance, because, for the first time in years, I'm actually going to show up somewhere. Dance. Eat. Hang out. Try to have a good time.

"Try to relax. Worst case scenario, you use one of your wishes, right?"

"Yes, but I think I need to save my wishes for more important things than strapless gowns."

"Katherine, you amaze me. I've never met anyone like you. Please believe me when I say I'll figure something out. Now, head downtown."

I can't believe it, but I believe him. I really do. So

I turn toward downtown. When we're stopped at a light, I notice for the first time that he's still in the clothes I met him in. Poor guy, he looks like he owns a gym or something. Truth is, I like looking at Eugene in those short shorts and white t-shirt. I hope he never changes. Oh alright, I'll be kind.

"We should probably get you some clothes too, so you... fit in... around here. In fact, you'll need a shirt and tie for my reunion, if you're going?"

"I'll gladly attend with you. But you don't need to worry. I have a plan now."

"A good plan, or a half-assed plan?"

"I haven't been on this planet this long for nothing," He smiles. "It's a very good plan. Just you wait."

HALF AN HOUR LATER, we're parked in front of a luxury apartment building.

"This is it. This is the place," he says, and we go inside. At the intercom, Eugene hits a button and it makes a buzzing sound. He waves up at a camera and mumbles into the speaker.

"Ginnifer. It's me."

"*Gin*-nifer?" I stare at him blankly. "Not, *Jen*-nifer?"

"No, it's pronounced Gin-ih-fur. Ginnifer June."

"Oh, that's pretty. If you like stripper names.

Eugene! You're taking me to see a *stripper* when we have serious shopping to do?"

"Just wait. Wait until you see her." *Buzz*. The glass door unlocks, and Eugene opens it for me. "After you, Princess."

"Enough. You don't have to be so dramatic." This can't be a dream, because I know I woke up this morning, but how'd I end up with a chivalrous genie, attending to my almost-every desire?

We take the elevator to the 18th floor, labelled Penthouse Suite on the elevator, and Eugene leads me to the door. He raises his hand to use the doorknocker, but it opens before his hand gets there.

"Eugenius! Honey!" The woman standing before us looks like a ballerina. It's not just her physique, or the way she's twisted her blonde hair in a perfect bun at the back. She's dressed in a pink tutu, pink leotard, white tights, and ballet slippers. And she sparkles. That's the best way to describe her. Her face sparkles, her leotard sparkles, even her hair sparkles, with a stunning, youthful glow. What is that product? I want it. I want it now!

"What have they done to you this time? Gold's Gym, huh? You look great!" Ginnifer opens her arms wide and wraps Eugene in a warm hug. They hug a long time. Eventually, she lets us inside.

"Come in, come in, I hear we have work to do."

"Hear? But. But… Eugene, did you borrow my cell when I was driving? I didn't notice…"

"I'm a genie, Katherine, remember? I don't need cell phones. All I need is magic." He looks sheepish, and adds, "Okay, yes, I texted her on your cell. Thanks." A texting genie. I shake my head and look at Ginnifer.

"Well, you two have come to the right place, because Eugene and I make beautiful magic together!" Ginnifer laughs and squeezes Eugene's hand. I feel a pang of jealousy. He and Glittery Gal have a past?

Ginnifer sits down on the white couch across the room and motions for us to sit beside her in two cosy-looking white arm chairs.

Eugene makes the introduction. "Katherine, this beautiful creature is Ginnfer June. She'll be your Fairy Godmother for the day."

I have fallen down the rabbit hole. I've fallen, and I can't get out. *What* did Gram put in my tea the other day?

"My Fairy Godmother? Oh right. Of course. Because when a genie pops out of your Wii, it's only common practice to visit your Fairy Godmother in her Penthouse Suite next."

"Oh sweetie," Ginnifer laughs. "I'm not a real Fairy Godmother. Just, in a manner of speaking!"

"Ginny was my fifth gig as a genie," Eugene explains. "She'd lived her entire life in poverty. When I found her, she was living on the streets. After much disbelief in my abilities, like you, she finally wished to become a ballerina. Then she wished for this luxury apartment, and then, she wished for the closet of her dreams. She's one of my few Masters who asked for material things, but managed to keep a pure heart and good intentions." He smiles at her.

Ginny stands up and takes my hand. "Ah yes, I do love to share the wealth. Get up, honey. Let me show you something." She leads me to a set of gold-rimmed glass French doors, swings them open, and claps her hands. Several pot lights turn on, revealing a bright, white room three times the size of my bedroom. There are gold-plated shelves wrapped around its perimeter, starting at the floor and ending at the ceiling. Placed neatly upon these shelves are rows and rows of beautiful shoes. Heels, runners, runners with heels – simply thousands of pairs of shoes.

"Do you believe in magic now?" she giggles.

I laugh out loud in both joy and disbelief. "What I believe is that you have shoes to fit every woman's parched soul in here. I'm not gonna knock that!"

"Here, these rows should be your size," Ginny says, and I get down on my knees and select several pairs of shoes at once. When I'm holding four pairs, two shoes fall out of my hands. If this is a dream, please don't wake me up, and also, please, please don't let me be snoring and drooling on the carpet in a Walmart change room.

"Take your time, you can try them all. You can take whichever ones you want," Ginny says.

"Can I come back next week?" I laugh as I try to squeeze on a pair of strappy silver heels. They're too tight.

Eugene is standing against a bare wall. "Here, try this," he says, and he hands me a gorgeous gold stiletto.

I stop what I'm doing and look up at him. "Why the special treatment? Why not make me use my three wishes and be done with me?"

"Because I like you," he says, and he doesn't even whisper it. Ginny smiles and leaves the room. "Because you're the first Master I've had since Ginnifer who has actually listened to my story and taken interest in who I am, and where I came from. Because, I think we're friends, and friends help friends in need."

I can feel my cheeks getting hot. I look down at my right foot, where I've placed the gold stiletto. It's a perfect fit.

"Okay, my friend," I whisper. "Thank you." That's all I can come up with. I hope he knows I'm sincere. "Any idea where the other shoe is?"

"I'd ask the prince," Eugene looks right at me.

"There's a prince too? Jeez, where does this thing end?"

"I was kidding! No! You can relax. I'm the only magical person you're gonna meet. Here!" he chuckles and hands me the other gold shoe.

I'm not sure where it came from. I'm not sure

where he came from. And right now, I don't care. I've lived my whole life trying to make up for my mistakes; mistakes that weren't all mine in the first place. Maybe it's time I started living.

The shoe fits.

I'M WALKING around Ginny's apartment in a pair of sparkly, gold stilettos and a gold, strapless, above-the-knee gown. I take one last, highly-unladylike slurp of the strawberry-banana smoothie she made me. I feel six feet tall. That's probably because these are five-inch heels. But I also feel beautiful and more confident since spending the afternoon with these wonderfully odd, magical people.

"I think this is it," I smile at Ginny.

"Okay, let's have a look at you, dear." Ginny takes a finger and motions for me to turn around, and I follow her instructions with my body, letting the gown's short skirt balloon out as I twirl around in a full circle.

"I do believe we've found your dress, Katherine," Ginny says, and claps her hands together like an enthusiastic child on Christmas morning.

"You're stunning." I hear his voice from across the room. Eugene is in the kitchen doorway, raising his water glass in my direction. The scene would be like something out of a movie: the dapper gentleman swooning over the Cinderella-turned-Princess, except, he's still wearing those red shorts and that gym t-shirt.

Ginny looks his way, studies him a moment, and seems to read my mind. "And now, Eugenius; now it's your turn."

"Me? Oh, no no. No. I'm not big on dressing up," he replies, but Ginny isn't listening.

Ginny opens another gold-plated closet beside the first one. This one is full of man-clothes. I wasn't kidding, I'm going to have to get Ginny's number and bring my girls here next week.

Eugene disappears into the closet. Well, it's more like Ginny pushes him inside, with him resisting as best he can, groaning and muttering under his breath. Even with her pushing him with all her might, she manages to look regal. She wears a demure look on her face, and reminds me of Princess Kate. Mind you, she's in a shimmery pink tutu. Kind of spoils the illusion. But pretend Fairy Godmother or poor woman who found her riches, she has my utmost respect for what happens next.

Eugene steps out of the closet.

I'm relieved I put that smoothie down on the coffee table, or else I'd have had to contend with strawberry banana flavoured push-up boobs for the rest of the evening. Come to think of it, most of the boys I knew in high school would rather enjoy that. But I digress.

Eugene is a movie star on Oscar night. His jet

black hair is combed back, leaving a sexy James-Dean style wave at the front. His black tux is a surprise, and I love the look on him. He's wearing a white shirt, with the top two buttons left open, and no bow-tie. It's a casual elegance; an entirely freeing look. I completely get why Ginny chose it for him.

James Deanius walks over to the wall-to-wall mirrors across the room and checks his reflection. I notice a discreet nod of approval.

"Ginnifer. I do like this. Thank you."

"You can keep it, Eugenius. I owe you one. Many, actually, for getting me off the streets and living this life." She comes up behind him, wraps her arms around his stomach, and hugs him as she looks at him in the mirror.

I really feel like I'm interrupting something. I'm not sure what, but I don't feel comfortable standing here staring. Damn. I thought we had something special happening between us. I guess, once again, the fat girl with low self-esteem only saw what she wanted to see.

I pick up the small gold clutch purse Ginny picked out for me and turn to leave. I'll make my way to the reunion on my own. I open the clutch and check my cell for the time. I have a half hour to get there.

"Katherine! Wait! You're forgetting your date!" Eugene breaks away from Ginny and steps in front of me, opening the front door.

"After you, Princess," he says and places his hand

at the small of my back as I walk on through. I must remember never to tell him what that does to me. My knees buckle, but I regain strength within seconds, so he doesn't notice.

"Seriously, Eugene, just call me Katherine."

"Fine, but you should call me Gene," he says.

Gene. I love that.

Your carriage awaits you, Katherine." He smirks, and presses the elevator button for us. Ginny is walking behind us, beaming.

"I'm so happy for you two. I hope you get everything you wish for."

"Oh, she's doing all the wishing. I'm just along for the ride." Gene smiles.

"Thanks again!" I say, as the elevator doors start to close, adding with a giggle, "Fairy Godmother!"

By now, it's no surprise that everything around her sparkles, especially her eyes, as she winks, and gives me a wave.

IO

"Ooga Chucka, Ooga Chucka. I can't stop this feelin', deep inside of me…"

We're just getting our seatbelts on when my cell phone starts ringing that ridiculous tune that I'd chosen as my ring tone. What is it called again? Right. *Hooked On A Feeling*. Blue Swede.

Crap! Crap! It's Jenna. What time is it? I'm supposed to pick the girls up at the gym.

I fumble around my purse, find the phone, and open it.

"Mom. Where are you? It's six-forty-five. You're supposed to be here."

"Honey, I'm so sorry, it's just that I decided to go to my reunion at the last minute. It's… it's just something I need to do for myself. Do you think you can stay with your cousins one more night?"

"Yes. We have fun there."

"Was that a dig? Jenna, I'm doing the best I can as a single mother… I even made excuses to keep you away from your father, who wanted to see you this weekend."

"Whatever, I don't get how you can't get out of bed, but you can dance at some stupid reunion."

"Jenna!" I can hear Alyssa trying to grab the phone from her sister. "I probably won't dance. But it's a start…"

"Mommy?" Alyssa's on the phone now. She sounds worried about me. "What are you doing? They're going to make fun of you. This isn't such a good idea of yours…"

"It's okay, sweetie. Things are… different now." I smile at Gene, who's sitting patiently beside me in the passenger seat. His brow is sweating. Must be hot in here in that tux.

"Things are going to be different from now on."

I think about all the times I missed dancing with my daughters because of my weight. The holidays that were ruined because I was too afraid of Jimmy. Christmas mornings when they tried to pull me up off the sofa so we could dance in a circle to *Happy Christmas (War Is Over)*. Oh, how I love that song. But I'd just sit there – with them each tugging on an arm, and shake my head. "No. Mommy can't."

I REMEMBER ONE EASTER, when we were sitting together peacefully, counting the eggs the girls had collected. Jimmy had been out all night, and came storming into the house, obviously hung-over, or still drunk. When he saw our youngest with chocolate all over her face and her hands, he snapped. "Why do you give them this sugary shit?" he yelled. "It's not good for them, and we can't afford it." Then he grabbed their rainbow-coloured baskets and dumped their contents in our garbage pail. The girls started wailing. My heart breaking, I sent them to their rooms for fear they'd see what was going to happen next.

Jimmy hit my face so hard that morning I nearly lost consciousness. I was on the kitchen floor, blood curling in a pool beneath my nose, and he was still sitting at the kitchen table, smoking and reading some stupid notice from the city about when we could water our lawn. He actually started talking to me about it as though it mattered, as though I cared, or should care.

"We can only water every second day. Don't forget." He tossed the notice on the floor near my head, got up from the table, and left the kitchen. I only sat up when I heard him slam the front door.

"YEAH WELL I'LL believe it when I see it," Jenna has grabbed her cell back and clearly wants to end the conversation. "We'll get Aunt Cici to drive us home tomorrow afternoon."

"Okay. Sweetie? I'm kind of in a hurry. Could you call Gram and let her know I'm going to be out late tonight? I think a call would be nicer than a text."

"Yeah, no problem. Um, thanks, about Jimmy. Thanks. Have fun, okay."

"Thanks, Jenna, I'll try." I feel a little relieved to hear her say thanks. Maybe we'll be okay once I turn my life around. I can get another job, now that I can move around more, and I can start doing stuff with my kids. I'm not sure how I'm going to explain this sudden weight loss to anyone in my family, though… I glance over at Gene. A long stream of sweat is dripping off his forehead.

"I'm so sorry, I had to touch base with my family. Open a window, and we'll get going."

"Everything okay?"

"I think it will be. I don't know how I'm going to explain this sudden weight-loss, though." I take the car out of park and start driving. When I look back in the rear view mirror, Ginny's apartment building isn't there. It's disappeared, and there's an empty lot in its place. I shake my head, but keep on driving. I'm going to have to get used to strange happenings.

"I've noticed, more and more in these last few decades," Gene says, "that the word 'miracle' is thrown around this planet like a beach ball on a windy day. Miracle treatment. Miracle skin. Miracle food. Why don't you just say you tried a 48-hour miracle diet? It'll be another day before you see them, right?"

"Because they'll think they should hospitalize me! No one loses this many pounds this fast!" I laugh.

"Yes, but if they see it, they'll believe it. Trust me, that's how it always works," Gene says, and then, from out of nowhere, a red rose appears in his hand. He places it on my lap. "I wasn't sure if you guys wore corsages to this kind of shindig. There's a vase for this in the backseat, so it should last at least a day."

"Oh, wow, this is so sweet." We pull into my old high school parking lot. Trudeau High. I can feel the hives on my chest rising, rising, rising. I want to scratch them. I want to pull out of the parking lot and drive away. Home. Fast.

"You can do this."

I'm not sure how Gene knows what I'm feeling. Or maybe the hives have already turned into that ugly red rash I always get on my chest when I'm nervous. He takes the rose from my left hand and puts it in a thin white vase on the backseat, then takes my right hand and squeezes it. "We can do this."

"Kay. Okay. Er, do I have a rash on my chest?" I look down but can't really make it out in this light. It's already getting dark. Must be past seven-thirty now.

"You're asking me to look at your chest?" He chuckles.

"Yes, yes, you have my permission. This one time." I laugh.

"It's fine, Katherine." He looks back up to my eyes. "You're beautiful."

I'm amazed at how two words from him can make me melt. I thought Gene must have felt hot in his tux, but now I'm ready to rip off my dress. And not just because his charm is turning me on, though it is. It's hot, and I'm nervous, and my heart is thumping with anticipation and joy, hard and fast, *ka thump ka thump ka THUMP*. I'm afraid it might burst out of my chest cavity.

"I'm really happy you came here with me tonight, Gene."

"I'm happy to be here, Petal. I hope it's all you want. I hope you show them."

"Petal?" I blush. "What happened to Princess?"

He puts a finger to my lips and draws on them lightly. I'm in heaven. "You're more delicate than I thought, but you're surprisingly strong. You're like a flower's petal. Can I call you that?" His hand moves to my bare shoulder.

"Yes." I can feel his face inching toward mine. I inch mine closer to his, and close my eyes. Yes, sure, I'd like that. Maybe even some tongue. Stop it, Cat, stop thinking and be in this moment!

Bang! Bang! Bang!

I open my eyes.

Crap. Someone is knocking on the car window. This is so annoying.

"Make-out sessions happen *later* people. The party's inside!"

It's someone I recognize, but I can't remember his name. He's in a suit and a purple tie, and his date is in a strapless, purple, above-the-knee gown. They're both incredibly drunk, trying to hold each other up, but not succeeding.

Suddenly, I remember his name. It's Top 40 Tom! Date #3 in my series of unfortunate dates, and probably my worst of them all, because we never actually managed to have a conversation, even though his language was, well, quite lyrical. God, I remember that date so clearly, for all the wrong reasons. It's a painful stretch of memory lane, and it almost ruined my album collection.

———

Tom stood at my doorway with a crooked smile and a bouquet of yellow roses in his hand.

What a nice start, for a change. No horrible odour, no outrageous polyester clothing, acceptable dental work… who said online dating doesn't work? This guy was even cute!

"Let's get this party started!" he announced. *Wow, keen, or just inappropriate?* Then I realized he was singing.

Kind of. Well, at least he hadn't said, "Who let the dogs out!"

Gram took the flowers and gave me a goodbye hug. "I'd better go put these in water. Probably really cheap ones, and they'll die if I don't," she grunted, hurrying off. I chuckled. *Way to remain positive, Gram.*

He opened the passenger door for me with, "Cause us tramps, baby, we were baw-un to ruuuun."

I gave him an awkward smile and got in, mourning the fact that as much as I love Springsteen, I can probably never listen to that song again.

We were on our way to the roller skating rink. I'd come up with the idea when I'd heard from the girls that they liked hanging out at Roll With It with their friends. I hadn't worn roller skates since I was a kid, and I was a little worried I'd trip all over the place, but restaurants had hardly worked for my previous dates. I'd decided to be brave and try something new.

Halfway there, we got stuck in traffic. There was no music playing and an awkward silence filled the car. Then I heard the low growl...

"I'm on a highway of hell..." Tom sang, and yet, he seemed to be smiling.

He glared at the cars ahead of him, then said to me, in a surprisingly good William Shatner impression, "Tell. Me. Why. I. Don't. Like. Tuesdays."

I grinned. *Huh, not too shabby, despite that he got the day wrong.* "Hey, that was good." I tell him.

I started to ask if he'd done theatre in the past, but

he interrupted, in that monotone voice, "I wanna shoot, oo oo oot, the whole day to pieces." He took his finger and shot a fake bullet through the windshield.

"Riiiiight," I hesitated. "That's sort of the next line, I can't remember…"

Tom pulled into the Roll With It parking lot and parked near the entrance. He was quiet as we walked into the building. He paid for my skate rental. I was too far away to hear, but I wondered if he actually spoke to the attendant, or if he used a line from a classic album. A minute later he led me toward the rink in silence. *Okay, quiet is fine. We're just getting used to each other.*

As we sat on a bench and laced up our skates, I tried to get the conversation flowing again.

"So tell me, you wrote in your profile that you've been married before. Did that end… er… badly?"

He had a grave expression on his face. He opened his mouth, but out came William Shatner's voice again. "I came in like a wrecked beach ball. I never hit so big at love."

"Okeee." I got up, faked a smile, and backed away from Top 40 Tom. It was getting weird.

I started to skate around the rink, but tripped within seconds, falling flat on my behind. *Ouch. Please don't come help me up. Please, just leave me alone, WackJob.*

Top 40 Tom was suddenly in front of me, holding both my elbows, easing me up to my feet. Then, he went for it, with gusto. He didn't sing, he spoke in a monotone voice, but I recognized the song immediately as the *Friends* theme song. *What is wrong with this guy? How did I not see crazy plastered all over his profile?*

"So no one told you life was gonna be this way. Your job's a mess, confess, you're DOA!"

"Gee, thanks, Tom, that's really kind of you. You know, I just remembered I left a pot boiling on the stove. How forgetful of me!" I got off the rink, rushed to grab a seat, and pulled off my skates. Tom followed.

"Don't leave me this way. I can't survive, can't stay alive without your love, oh baby, don't leave me this way, no." He bent down on one knee.

Is this guy for real? Maybe not. "Is this a joke? Who put you up to this? Cici? Did Cici do this?" I started chuckling nervously. *Please let this be a prank.*

"I'm a joker, I'm a midnight smoker," he called after me. I realized this was no prank, so I headed for the nearest washroom. Once inside a locked cubicle, I pulled my cell phone out of my purse and dialed home. Gram answered.

"911. Dating 911!" I said. She knew the drill.

"We'll be right there."

I hid in the washroom until Gram and the girls came to rescue me, and we slipped out of a side door. I suspected Tom sang his way home to a Stones' song. *I can't get no. Sat-is-fac-tion.*

Top 40 Tom finally leaves my window, looking for his drunken date. I can hear him talking to her when he finds her, face flat against the trunk of our car.

"Let's get this started, ha!"

She laughs, trips over the back of our car, and they stumble off together into the sunset.

Gene looks at me, glances at the car radio clock and starts to open his door.

"So. Shall we go?"

I'm nervous. Everyone has noticed my fat first for so long, I'm not sure what I'm going to feel like when they notice my smile, my eyes, or my personality first, if they do notice those. Maybe they'll just look for the fat. Ask me to do a twirl to see where I've hidden it. Hell, I'm not sure I'm exciting enough anymore for my personality to be noticed first. Am I? I open my mouth to tell Gene to take me home, but he's already at my door, taking my hand.

"Come. Make an entrance, Katherine. You deserve this moment."

We go inside and reach the gymnasium doors, which have been left wide open. The theme is a clever "Back To The Future". There's a beat-up DeLorean on stage, and Huey Lewis and the News' "The Power of Love," is playing through the speakers when we walk in. I stand with Gene just inside the room's centre, basking in the moment. I look good, I feel fantastic, and I'm with a very good-looking man. I feel all eyes on me.

From the far end of the room, I notice Cathy Hollows put her drink down on the snack table, and leave her husband, Jake Hampton's, side. Jake stays behind, flirting with two women who are hanging onto his arms like accessories. The way the lighting moves from above, it's easy to see her walking to the centre of the gym to catch a glimpse of me, but she stands behind someone tall, thinking she's being discreet. She stares at us for a long time. A lot of people do. Then someone finally walks up to us.

"Cat? You look… fabulous! Really! Wow!" It's Angie. She wasn't ever especially mean to me; just never tried hard to be nice, either. She takes my hand and bends in for a kiss against my cheek, and I introduce Gene as my boyfriend. She looks impressed.

As Angie and Gene make small talk, I notice her glancing across the room at Cathy. Cathy grins back at her from the back of the gym, then scrunches her nose, and whispers something to the woman beside her. What have they been saying about me? Twenty years later, and they still need to find something to criticize, despite that I've lost a bunch of weight, and I'm wearing this stunning outfit? They'll never change. Never.

Suddenly, it doesn't matter anymore. I don't care what some drunken 40-year-olds think. I don't care what Cathy thinks! I care what my kids think. What

Cici thinks. What Gram thinks. And, surprisingly, I care what this dude who appeared from out of my Wii thinks. But these people, they don't care about me. They don't have my back like Gene and my family do. Why should I care about them?

"So, can I get you something to eat over there?" Gene takes my hand.

"No. Change of plans." I turn on my heels and lead him away, far, far away, from my past.

THE BURGER's delicious sauce is dripping down my chin and onto the napkin on my lap, but I keep on biting into the bun. I hear Gene laughing beside me, and I start laughing so hard, I have to put the burger down.

This diner is a throwback to the 50s, and it's done pretty well. If a camera crew came in right now and shot the scene in black and white, we'd look like a couple of kids in their prom clothes being served milkshakes in tall glasses, by a girl wearing white roller-skates. Okay, I guess I wouldn't actually pass for a high school graduate. But the rest is true.

We're seated side by side at the red and black checkered bar on silver stools covered in red leather. Gene takes my hand. How sweet. Then he lifts it and uses it to wipe the side of my mouth.

"You've got a little something there," he chuckles.

"But don't let me disturb your eating. You were on a roll there. Shall I order another four burgers?"

"Oh, no, you're right. I have to watch what I eat…" Then I catch a glance of my reflection in the glass window, and remember I'm not Fat Cat anymore. Dammit, he's going down for this!

"Gene! I can finally eat what I want and not worry about people staring at me while I eat. It's refreshing."

"As were your two milkshakes, I bet." He gestures to the empty glasses by my side. There's a twinkle in his eye. I hadn't realized until now how much he likes to show affection by teasing. I can get used to this.

"Okay, okay, Bad Cop, I realize I can't eat like this all the time. Gimme a break, we just ditched my reunion."

"Ah yes, and why did we do that again?"

"I realized I didn't need to prove anything to anyone anymore. I just need to prove a few things to myself."

"That's quite mature, coming from a gal who had a couple straws up her nose a few moments ago." He laughs.

"You started it."

Our laughter echoes across the diner. It's one of the most beautiful sounds I've heard in a long time. We're completely alone, except for the waitress and cook in the back. There's no one else listening to us, and no one watching. I can feel Gene leaning in for a kiss; our kiss that was rudely interrupted a few hours ago.

I lean in with enthusiasm, look into his mesmerizing green eyes, accidentally twirl the other way on the stool, lose my balance, and fall flat on my ass onto the cold diner floor.

"Crap!"

I have dress up to my chin. I'm glad I wore granny panties, because I'm certain the waitress and cook, who have run to help me up, will notice my flushed red cheeks, and both my other cheeks as well. Shit. Granny panties. Gene just saw those. What colour were they again? Maybe he didn't notice.

I study his amused face once the cook has helped me back up onto my stool. Yup, he saw the granny panties.

"You okay there, humpty dumpty?"

I'm fuming. Seriously, a little empathy here? I slide off the stool, grab my purse off the bar, and turn to walk out of the diner. I don't need to take this teasing. I had enough of that in high school.

I feel his gentle hand curve around my shoulder.

"Hey! It was a term of endearment!" He turns my body around and pulls me close to him. I can feel my knees buckling under me. I decide to let them buckle.

"You hear that? I'm endeared to you, Katherine."

His lips meet mine, and the room starts spinning. The kiss takes me on a roller coaster ride; dancing in the spotlight, swinging high on the big kid swings. It throws me off balance, then wraps me in a warm blanket, leaving me in soft sand by the ocean.

"Wow," I mutter, and open my eyes, wishing I could come up with something that sounds slightly more intelligent.

"Wow, back," he grins and squeezes my hand.

"Ahem." The waitress on skates is right behind us. "Your bill?"

Gene reaches out for the bill, but I snatch it from his hands.

"It's on me. You got me the dress, the shoes, the wish. It's the least I can do."

Gene chuckles loudly as he opens the diner door for me. "Okay, but don't just think you can have your way with me now that you've bought me dinner. I'm not that kind of genie."

I pout. "Not even just a little?"

His left eyebrow raises higher than I've ever seen it rise before. He opens the driver's car door and gestures for me to get in. When he touches my lower back, shivers and heat rise from the bottom of my spine, through my breasts, up to my lungs, breeding a warmth and energy I haven't felt in years. His hands, his voice, are a hot stone massage.

"Exactly how fast can you drive us home?"

"God!"

Inhale, blow your hair out of your eyes.

"This is—"

Quick, get more breath in before you fall over.

"Amazing. I haven't had sex in—"

Yes! Yes! Yes!

"Years!"

I'm so overjoyed, I'm laughing. Out loud. Sitting on top of him, and laughing. God, I hope he doesn't think I'm laughing at him.

"Tell me about it. Try, two-thousand years!" Gene says, and manages to laugh too, despite that he's also out of breath.

Our bodies move together like beautiful music. Okay, maybe not beautiful. Maybe not music. More like awkward penguins sliding down a snow bank, racing each other to the water. We don't look anything like they do in the movies. But it feels fantastic.

I'm holding onto the bed's headboard for support, rising and falling, up and down, up and down, arching my back. My head has fallen back; my hair has fallen down. I'm lost in ecstasy. Gene smiles and starts to roll to the left, and I roll with him, so I'm under him.

He moves to kiss my lips, and I move up to meet him, but our noses get in the way. "Ouch!" he says, and I can't help laughing again.

He tries to recover from all that awkwardness and does a damn good job of it. Soon, I'm grabbing the sides of the bed and moaning, "Yes! Yes!"

Suddenly, he has an intense look on his face. Uh oh.

Don't finish yet. Don't finish yet, just…Oh. He finished yet.

"Uh, Katherine, I'm sorry," he pants, and falls down on the bed beside me. "That's the problem with bottling it all up – literally bottling it up – all those years."

I chuckle. It really doesn't matter. I turn toward him, so I'm lying sideways, and rub his back. "It's okay. I'm just so happy we did that."

He leans in closer and tenderly kisses my eyebrows, my nose, my lips. I just lie there soaking all the love in, like a sponge taking in water. This is where I want to be forever. With him. Like this. Just being real.

I turn my head to the left to catch a glimpse of our bodies entwined, in the mirror.

Oh no! No! No!

It's me, but it's not. It's fat me again. Panic rises up from my stomach to my throat. It comes out in a loud, screechy sound.

"Gene! What have you done?"

"What do you mean, Petal?" He lies still, caressing my cheek.

"What's happened to me? I'm fat again! So what, you made me thin because you couldn't bear to make love to disgusting me?"

"Katherine." He sits up. He seems breathless for another reason now. His eyes are filled with concern.

"No, never. You getting your old body back – that happened an hour ago, when we were starting this. I could tell you hadn't noticed, and well, you were having so much fun, I didn't think you needed to know just yet. I was having fun, too. So I didn't think much about it, actually."

"You made love to me looking like… this? I... I…" I'm humiliated, and confused. Where'd my beautiful body go?

"Katherine. I like you. Everything about you. *You*. Don't you get it? I've never met anyone like you. I wouldn't dare hurt you."

I stand up and quickly put on the robe I find hanging at the far end of my closet. The 'fat' end. I notice one of the 'thin' nightgowns Gene had surprised me with hanging at the other end of the closet. Taunting me.

"That's very sweet, but it doesn't bring my good body back. What kind of genie are you anyway? You give out dreams, then take them away? Is this your idea of a good time?"

Gene sighs, picks up his pants off the floor, and quickly pulls them on. He sits on the edge of the bed and looks up at me with pleading eyes.

"I didn't plan this. I didn't know it wasn't going to stick, but I had my suspicions."

"Wasn't going to *stick*? You had your suspicions? You're the worst genie I've ever met!" I scream and throw a pillow at him. It feels so good, I pick it up and start whacking him over the head with it, repeatedly.

"Stop! Please, just stop!" He doesn't raise his voice, push me, or hit me. He just asks me to stop.

Huh.

"I'm not infallible. Sure, I've got magic, but magic isn't infallible, either. I thought when you asked to be thin for your reunion that we might run into this problem. You should have asked to be thin for the rest of your life. But I didn't want to worry you once you'd already wished your wish. I wanted you to enjoy every minute of it."

"I did, but now it's over, and I'm fat, and we're back to square one, and you should have warned me! You should have warned me this would end! Go back to the Kardashian sisters!

"What kind of genie *are* you anyway?" I know I'm repeating myself, but I can't help that. I always do that when I'm enraged.

I pull on new panties, grab my favourite big t-shirt from my closet, slip on my fuzzy socks and stomp out of my room and slam the door, but not before I hear the smallest, softest, most defeated voice I've ever heard, muttering, "Not the very good kind, it would seem. Not very good at all."

I hear it, and I want to turn back and forgive him, but I gather up all my rage from my life with Jimmy, from losing Ben and every other loss, and keep on walking. I'm not letting another man hurt me again. Never again.

I get two paces out the door. Gram is standing in front of me in the hallway, a flashlight in her hand.

"Everything okay, dear? You and Loverboy not getting along?"

"Gram! When, when, did you get home?" I stammer. "Are the girls in, too?"

"No, just me, no worries. Pretty sure I'm the only one who heard you two doing the horizontal mambo."

"Oh, Gram." I fall into her arms, laughing and sobbing all at once.

II

I'm sitting on Gram's bed, drinking the herbal tea she made me. Love this Lemon zinger. She's sitting back in a white leather easy chair, her feet propped up on a white leather ottoman. I could relax into this, except for the fact that Gram's face is covered in tiny rectangles of multi-coloured light. And they keep moving: across her face, onto the wall, across her face, onto the wall. It's making me dizzy.

"Gram, you think you can you turn that thing off?"

"Oh, right, it lulls me to sleep, so, I forget about it," she leans over to a socket on the wall and pulls the plug on the large disco ball rotating where the ceiling fan used to be, above us.

"You fall asleep to a disco ball?"

"That, and this, dearie," and she presses a small

remote in her hand and leans farther back into her chair. "Sigh… They're just so dreamy."

Suddenly, three high-pitched voices singing, *"Nobody gets too much love anymore,"* come wailing into the room from speakers in three of the four corners of Gram's ceiling. If ever there were a poster child for Bee Gee Fever, it would be my Gram. She stands up, closes her eyes, and starts swaying to the music. After a few minutes, the song changes to *"Stayin' Alive."* Her eyes open wide, she puts her hand on one hip, and begins lifting it up and down to the beat.

"Gram, you fall asleep to Stayin' Alive?" I shout above the music.

"Sure do. At my age, it's good to be reminded of what you're supposed to do during the night. When I'm still kickin' around the next morning, I thank Barry and Robin and Maurice."

I stifle a laugh, because I don't think she's trying to be funny, then realize if we're going to have a serious discussion, I'm going to have to be the wet blanket here.

"Gram," I shout above the music. "That's very nice and all, but do you think you can turn it down just a little?"

"Sure." She sits back down, turns the music off, and puts down the remote. "This doesn't usually bother you. What's wrong?"

I've always loved how she never misses a beat,

never minces words. But I'm not sure I'm ready to talk about this yet.

I thought I could trust Gene, but I'm starting to wonder if he's just a fraud. Maybe he gave me some weird diet pill that works instantly. Maybe he's just a guy who's been looking for a place to stay, and a vulnerable woman in his bed.

If that's the case, I've been a hell of a lot of work. It would have been easier to pick up someone in a bar. I mean, why'd he help me stand up to Jimmy? Why'd he buy new clothes for me, open doors for me; give me a fairy-tale day at Ginny's? Why'd he touch me like he loved me? And how do you explain the purple smoke?

"Gram, it's complicated. *Really complicated.* But this thing with Gene moved fast, because, well, I thought I had something special with him, that's all. Now I realize I've been conned by love, once again."

She leans in. "Oh, the love con, huh. Yeah. Love is bigger than you. It'll beat the crap outta you, too, but you hear bells and get up for round two, thinkin' it's gonna be different."

"I didn't believe it could ever be different. Not after Jimmy. I didn't think I'd ever open up to someone again. Gene has changed that." I stop talking a moment and take a deep breath. "I just don't know if he's for real, Gram."

"Trust your instincts, hon. Jimmy, well, he's not

your typical man. You gotta believe that, and move on. Some people are just born assholes."

I can't help but laugh out loud at that one. She smiles at me, and as she leans back again, her hand hits the keyboard on the table beside her. The computer I bought her a few years ago wakes up, and I notice she's on a Twitter account, a hot pink leopard print as its background. Then I notice the title. @BadAssGrandma. You've got to be kidding me.

"You Tweet? Gram? Seriously?" I spit some of my herbal tea back out into its cup. Gross. But better than spewing it all over the bed, which I almost did.

"Yeah, 'bout six months now. Jenna showed me how. I got curious and set up this here account. Gotta keep the old upstairs clear of cobwebs; keep social. Twitter does that for me."

"Wow. Look at your following!" 2,000-some people, following my Gram. I can't believe this. I don't even use Facebook, but my 91-year-old grandmother Tweets.

"Can't believe how informal it all is. Especially how women bare their souls on there. Was a time we had to call our husbands 'sir'. Now, we Tweet about their penis size. If I were a guy, I'd be looking for life on another planet."

I shake my head, chuckling at her wit, and what she's gotten herself into, once again. "I think Twitter is the least of men's problems, Gram. Once we entered the workforce, all bets were off. They don't know whether to open a door for us, ask for our number, give us their number, play it cool, or sext message us. The game has changed, and the rules are foggy. None of it makes sense anymore."

"Well, welcome to life. Life don't make sense, no matter how old you get. Just don't hurt people, learn to laugh at yourself, and do the nasty like there's no tomorrow."

"I'm doing all those things, Gram. All those things. But what do I do about Gene?"

"You want to kick him out?"

"Not sure. He…well, he promised me one thing, and did another."

"Was it intentional?" She looks me right in the eye. God, Gram, how can you get it, so quick? Amazing.

"No. Gram. No. I guess not. He's not like that."

"Well, then, I guess you best be goin' downstairs and doing some mending. Just don't be so loud and bouncy about it this time. That old bed won't last forever."

She bends down, picks something up off the carpet, and throws it my way. It's a t-shirt. Her t-shirt. I open it up, and without thinking much, place it on my chest. Then I look down to read the words. It says:

"I Wanna Take A Ride On Your Disco Stick."

I laugh out loud. "Classy, Gram. Classy." But I'm grinning. She beams back at me.

"Okay, I'll go back and talk to Gene. I'll give it a

try." I stand up and bend down to give her a quick hug and kiss on the cheek, then start to leave. "I, um, hey. Can you help me learn to Tweet? I'd love to meet more people online… but no more online dating!"

"You bet. So long as you follow me," she grins.

"Gram, wherever you lead, I'll follow. It's always been our way." I smile, and as I close her door, I say, "Don't forget your meds, and don't stay up too late."

"You're not my Mom," she barks, but I can hear her chuckling. Oh, the t-shirt. I forgot. I open the door one more time, and throw it at her head.

"Hey! That's elderly abuse!" She laughs.

"Goodnight, Gram," I say, closing the door behind me.

Now. What am I going to do about Gene?

GENE IS SITTING at the kitchen table, digging into a bag of salt and vinegar chips like there's buried treasure at the bottom.

"I thought you were above junk food. I thought you told me it was crap for my body." I go to the fridge, grab a diet cola, open it, and lean against the counter.

"I did, but this is my body, not yours, and by the sounds of it, I don't have to answer to you anymore," he mutters. He's clearly not happy.

"Damn!" He slams the chips down on the table.

"Do you have to go and ruin a perfectly good snack too?"

My better mind says I should walk away before this turns ugly, but for some reason, I pull up a chair and keep listening.

"I mean, I was minding my business as a dormant genie, and along comes you. You with your dreams and your openness and honesty, and you make me – you make me tongue tied and frustrated, and so much lighter than ever before. You make me want to be free again."

I have to catch my breath before I respond. "So you toyed with me because you wanted me?"

"For God's sakes, Katherine. I wasn't toying with you. Not one bit." He sighs. "I didn't know the wish wouldn't last more than a day. It was a mistake, okay? Are you even listening?" He runs his hands through his hair, then grabs my soda and takes a long gulp.

"I made a mistake not telling you exactly what to say. Do you allow for mistakes, or are you going to send me back to the darkness, because I'm a good for nothing genie?"

"Do I allow for mistakes?" I repeat, hesitate, then blurt out, "My whole life has been a mistake, one awful mistake after another!" I can't help it, the dam has broken. I'm sobbing now.

Gene reaches out his hand to mine, but doesn't take it. "Oh. Don't cry, Katherine, please, don't cry. I hate seeing you cry." He pulls himself closer to me, and gently wipes a tear off my cheek. When I look over at him, all my anger melts away, but the tears fall harder. I take his hand in mine.

"I don't think losing the weight is going to change how I feel about myself, anyway. I need to change what happened the night of Ben and Jake's drag race. I wish I could be in a happier place, with happier memories. Take me back to the day of Ben's accident so I can make it right."

Suddenly, the table starts shaking. Plates and glasses are rattling in the cupboards. Crap. Great timing. It's an earthquake. Wait. There's purple smoke rising from under the table, under our hands, and out from under Gene.

"Oh. My God. I... I?" I shout above the noise.

"Yes, sweetheart, yes you did," he shouts back above the noise. "And, I'm so sorry I have to do this, but this next part? It's embarrassing, but it's in my job description." He stands up and says something else, more quietly, but all I can make out amid the purple haze is his haggard expression.

"Your wish is my command!"

12

His eyes say so much. They say that he's said this a million times, and that he's bored with saying it. They also tell me he's not afraid for what's about to happen next. He wraps his arms around me tight, and pulls me in close as we begin to spin in circles. We're spinning and spinning, faster and faster, rising and rising off the ground, and all I can make out is purple smoke, and Gene's green eyes coming at me, over and over again. It's like the Twirl-A-Whirl at the CNE, only I have no clue where we're going, and we aren't strapped in.

I hold onto him. I hold onto him, remembering all the good he has done, and how safe he's made me feel. I can feel his hands tight against the back of my head and lower back. We're twirling so fast, I can't see anything around us, but I can tell we aren't in my house anymore. We're in a vortex of purple smoke, and we're gaining altitude.

I feel like I'm in an airplane with the seatbelt sign still on, only there's no sweet attendant offering me snacks.

The turbulence has been constant, but suddenly, it just stops. The smoke begins to clear, and I feel Gene lighten his grip on me. We start floating downward, as though coming in for a landing. Now I can feel the ground under my feet.

Dirt. My feet are standing on dirt and moss. There's a beaten path off to my right, and ahead of me, I see the edge of a cliff, and below that, hundreds of tiny rooftops, and blue sky. Where the hell are we? I grab hold of Gene's arms and bury my face in his chest. At least we have his magic. At least there's that.

"*Where* in hell's name have we landed?"

Gene lets go of me, walks toward the cliff's edge and shouts into the empty space ahead. He turns back toward me and runs his hands through his hair. His face is white.

"Gene. This isn't reassuring me. Stop looking so panicked."

"Katherine, I'm not panicked. I'm confused. There's a difference."

"Neither one is very good."

"No, that's very observant of you, this isn't good,"

he snaps, as he kicks up some dirt, then bends down, grabs a small stone and whips it over the cliff in anger. I can hear it hitting other rocks on its way down.

I stare at him a moment, frowning. He stares back. His face softens when he sees my tears, and he walks back to me, taking my hand. "I'm sorry. I don't know where we are. At all." He points to a castle wall just ahead of us. "That looks like a ruin. Humour me here. Were there castle ruins in your small town in 1993?"

I can't help but laugh. If you counted Mr. Castle's house, just down the street from us, I suppose the answer would be yes. Mr. Castle was an odd old man who lived in a century-old building that was falling apart. Every summer when Gram and I went by on our bikes, without fail, he'd wave and call us over to try out his 'Orange tomato spread,' made with his prized, home grown tomatoes. Gram told me that Mr. Castle's wife had died tragically, and that we should show some respect, mind our manners, and eat this spread he so desperately wanted us to test on saltine crackers. The only problem was I detested tomatoes. I usually managed to spit half of it into the napkin when Mr. Castle wasn't looking, and thankfully, he always had watermelon out, so I washed the awful taste away with a slice or two.

Mr. Castle died in the summer of 1989. His house should have been condemned after that, but it never was. One night, Ben and I climbed through a badly boarded up window to check it out. We found an old piano in the living room, and Ben decided to dust off the bench, sit down, and play me a tune. "Roll Out the Barrell." It was so out of tune, though, I had to scream at him to stop playing, and he wouldn't stop. He kept laughing and playing, acting like a bar room entertainer, trying to annoy me.

I ran upstairs to get away from the noise, and felt shivers down my spine the minute I got to the top. There, at the end of the hallway, was Mr. Castle. He was holding out a plate of watermelon, and grinning at me. Just watermelon. No tomato spread. *Did he know, all those years? And still made me try it? That Devil!* I chuckled. I started to walk towards him. I didn't feel creeped out at all. I was about to reach out and grab a slice, when he just disappeared. He was there, in his plaid flannel shirt, overalls, and gardening gloves, and then, he was gone. I never told Ben. He would have teased me forever, and besides, for some reason, I wanted to keep it between me and Mr. Castle. Now, though, whenever I hear, "Roll Out the Barrell," I always think about that night, and what I saw.

"No, Gene," I say softly, pulling him by the hand toward the castle ruin." "No, this is definitely not in my home town. But I see a sign over there. Let's go check it out."

When we get to the sign, we realize it's for tourist information. The entire description is in French.

Wha? France? Has he seriously taken us off the North American continent?

We start reading the sign in silence. I scan it quickly at first, then read more carefully:

Cette falaise a une haute de 137 mètres… une sentinelle semble protéger le village médiéval de Mornas…une vue à vous couper le souffle…

I read on and learn the castle was built in the mid-12th century, and that once, in the 15th century, women and children were locked inside and massacred. Nice. Maybe I'll skip that part.

"Okay, my French isn't that great," I turn to Gene, "but I'm pretty sure we're in Mornas, at a medieval castle, overlooking the Rhone valley, on a cliff that's 137 metres high. And it's a tourist attraction. This is good! We can explore it a little, and then be on our way, back to 1993." See. I'm putting a positive spin on this. It's the overseas vacation I've never had.

Gene looks down at his feet and frowns. "Katherine, you're very kind to try to make the most of this, but the thing is, we shouldn't even be here. I'm not a very good genie." He starts walking through a door that leads into the open-roofed castle, and I follow. Inside, there's a wood platform with a throne on it, and a guillotine for tourist photo-ops. Gene sticks his head inside the guillotine, facing me.

"The thing is, I was afraid to tell you, but I'm actually a failed genie. Please. Just put me out of my misery right now."

I crack up. It isn't the reaction he's looking for. He pulls his head out of the guillotine, walks up to me, grabs my arms just beneath the shoulders, and looks me in the eyes.

"I'm serious, Katherine. I'm a failed genie. All these years, I've only had one success as a genie, and that was Ginnifer. They said I would stay in stasis forever if I didn't shape up and help someone else."

"Who is this 'they', Gene?"

"The voices when I'm in stasis."

"The voices? And I thought I needed therapy…"

"It's true. A group of voices tell me what to do and how to do it when I'm in stasis, and before I met you, they told me… about Logan and Ben. About how you needed to right your perceived wrongs. How I was to help you," he pauses and takes a deep breath. "And I sure as hell *wasn't* supposed to take you to a fucking fortress in France!"

He turns away, like he can't even face seeing my reaction. I sit down on the wooden throne and stare at my feet. So. I've been sent a FuckUp Genie. Figures. Yup. That so fits in with my life. I take a deep breath and collect my thoughts before speaking.

"What about the Kardashians? Trump? I thought they were success stories?"

He raises an eyebrow, and I hear a half chuckle. "No, sweetie. No. They only became famous after I stopped trying so hard to help them out."

"Oh. I see." His face is full of disappointment and

another emotion I really don't want him wearing any longer… shame. Suddenly, I want to help him as much as he wants to help me.

"I don't know how all the magic works, where it's coming from, and why we're both entwined in this, but we are, and I don't think giving up is the answer right now. So you messed up one of my wishes. So what – my first wish was a waste of time, too."

"I messed it up so much, I don't even know what year we're in right now. And even if exploring helps me get my bearings and gets you back to 1993," he lowers his eyes, "I don't know how we'd get back to your time, twenty years after that, with no wishes left." He starts to pace back and forth.

"Oh." I'd forgotten the wishes were limited. I stare at my hands. They're a little red – it's getting cold and windy. I just want to go home. This is such a colossal mess.

"But if we change things, can't I stay and live out that new… er… time line?"

"We'd need to return to your time to find out if we changed anything." He stops pacing and turns to look at me. "But we could go back to 1993 on one of my wishes," he says.

"You get wishes?"

"I get one. Only one. It's my freedom wish. I need to successfully help three Masters before I'm free, or, I can use my freedom wish after helping out two. But I think I owe you my wish, since I'm such a disaster, no?"

I chuckle. "I don't know, I married an alcoholic wife beater. I dropped out of a perfectly good business course. I tried to eat my way out of my guilt. I think we tie in the disaster department." We're both quiet for a minute, and in the silence, I make a realization.

"But, if we use your one wish, you may never be a free man…"

He puts his fingers to my lips, and is about to open his mouth, when our conversation is interrupted by the sound of cheering and clapping outside the castle walls, toward where I assume is the front entrance. We stop, look up to the sun, slowly lowering in the sky, and listen as the joyful noise fills our part of the castle. Gene breaks into a smile.

"I wonder if that's a good sign," he says. "We could use one right about now."

"Come on, let's go see what everyone's cheering about," I say, but he's already way ahead of me.

13

WHEN I CATCH UP WITH GENE AT THE FRONT DOORS of the castle, he isn't smiling anymore. They're closed. The cheering coming from the other side is growing more and more faint.

I try calling out, "Hey! Hey! We're still in here!"

No answer. We stand there, just staring at the large wooden doors until a few moments later, when we can't hear anyone anymore. Now, it's my turn to panic. I grab the large black handles on the castle doors and pull. They're locked. I don't want to believe this, so I keep on pulling. Finally, I feel Gene's hand on my shoulder.

"Katherine, it's no use. Look."

He points to the wall to the left of us. There's a large metal, digital clock. It reads 5:11.

"I'm not sure what year we're in," Gene sighs,

"but I suspect closing time is still five-o'clock. We're locked in here."

"*Fuckity!* When you mess up, you really mess up!" I move my shoulder away from his touch and go back to pulling on the door handle. It doesn't open. I try kicking it.

"Come on, be nice. I can fix this."

"Be nice? Be nice?! " I turn to look at him. "I thought you came into my life to help me. Instead, you've just made everything worse!"

"Oh and you're a fine cup of tea! You. You and your moods. And get with reality! I mean really, Princess, you wasted a whole wish on, essentially, going to a ball to show off your body! That's incredibly vain."

"Vain? Excuse me? I saw you eyeing yourself in that tux. You can't say I'm the only vain one here!"

"You're the only Princess here, that's for sure," he mutters, and starts kicking at the castle stones. He kicks high and low, and in between. He won't stop kicking. Dozens of pebbles crumble and start to fall to the ground, leaving small impressions on the castle wall. I watch him sweating and kicking, and kicking some more, and start to feel sorry that I was so hard on him.

"What are you looking at?" I ask, trying to sound kinder in my tone. He's putting his foot inside the impressions, as if they are steps.

He's been eyeing a garbage can over by one wall.

He walks over, rummages through it, and then looks behind it, bending down to pick something up. "Hey look. Someone tossed a wedding bouquet over here. It's fresh." He picks it up and gives it a whiff. "Mmm, love fresh red roses."

He picks up a thick yellow rope from behind the bin, and walks back to me with both the rope and the fragrant bouquet in his hand. He keeps the rope, but hands me the flowers, gesturing with a royal bow. "Bondage wedding?"

"I hear they're all the rage." I laugh. "So symbolic of what's ahead for the woman," I mutter into the flowers as I smell them, but I can tell he hears me, and chooses to ignore.

I notice a little tag on the bouquet of miniature red roses, and take a closer look at it. "May 4, 2017." That's today, but four years later. In the future. He's sent us to the future. I digest this, biting my cheek to avoid screaming. If I'm doing an inner-scream, imagine what Gene will do. He's going to lose that spark of hope I see in his eyes. I think I'll just keep this piece of information to myself.

"As odd as it is to find a rope here, it just might work," he says, and I can see the frustration fading from his eyes.

We're stuck in France, in the future. We can't even explore Paris. But something about the smell of these flowers and his stance, in those tight tuxedo pants, brightens my day. I find this very amusing. "You're going to try to rock-climb out of here? Up that wall? It's at least 50 feet high! And you're in a dress shirt and tuxedo pants!" I lean against the wall and start laughing.

Gene starts to laugh along with me, throwing the rope over his shoulder. "Listen, sweetheart, it seems I don't have much choice here, do I? Now, do you care to join me? I'll climb up to the top first, then try to pull you over. I'll throw this rope down for you to hang onto."

"Me? Climb? You've got to be kidding! I can't do that!" Besides that I haven't exercised in years, I'm still wearing a Bon Jovi "It's My Life" T shirt, and panties, and nothing else. That's not going to be a pretty view from the bottom.

"I'll do it if I have to, but why do we have to get out of here? Can't you just wish us back to 1993 right now?"

"You think I hadn't thought of that? I thought of that. I'm not stupid, Katherine," he grumbles down at me, but keeps climbing, panting, sweating.

I should be offended that he's snapping at me again, but my eyes are glued to his muscular behind right now. *Damn! He's hot! Gram was right.*

He keeps climbing, calling down to me. "I need better reception, okay? I seem to time travel best out in the wide open. No objects in my way. Okay, I'm almost ready for you." He grabs the top of the wall with one hand, turns toward me, and reaches out his other hand. "Your turn!"

"What if I'm not ready?" I breathe in and hesitate before saying, "You see how heavy I am. Is this wall going to hold me?"

He starts laughing again. "It's a stone wall. It will hold you! I have this rope for you to hang onto too. Come on. You can do this."

"Yeah well, can I just say, right now, in this moment, that you *suck*?"

"That was very grown up of you." He chuckles.

"It's true! If my first wish had stuck, I'd be home, thin, and probably eating cupcakes right now."

"Vanilla cupcakes, with sprinkles? Mmmm." He tries to change the subject, still motioning for me to start climbing.

"Yes, always with sprinkles. Gene! I'm not built to do this!"

"Take your time. Mornas wasn't built in a day!"

I chuckle, groan, put the red rose bouquet down on the ground, and put one socked foot into an impression on a lower stone. Who knew Dr. Scholl's spa socks could grip like this? I can't believe I'm doing this, and that I gave up perfectly good flowers for it as well. I place one hand on an upper stone and pull myself up. Stone after stone, I continue the same pattern, cursing under my breath the whole way up. Gene is cheering me on from above.

I'm doing this. I'm rock climbing an ancient wall. This is actually kinda cool.

"Tell you what, Petal, just grab this rope that's attached to my hand, wish us back to the right time from there, and that will do. I've got a clear view for miles and miles here, it should work fine now."

"You're joking, right?" I laugh. "I'm almost there, I'm not going to miss that view!" I grab onto the rope, but keep pushing myself harder. My fingertips feel raw and my lungs are on fire, but I keep pushing. *I'm almost there!*

When I finally let go of the rope and grab his hand, he pulls me up in one fell swoop, and firmly grabs onto my hips so I don't fall off the edge. Then he's kissing me. His face is salty from sweating and stubbly from the growth of his beard, but I don't care. It's the best feeling in the world.

"You did it! I knew you could!"

He kisses my eyebrows, and the tip of my nose. Not sure why he does that, but I love how it tickles. I smile up at him, then look out at the beautiful Rhone Valley below us. I've made it. We've made it.

"Sorry I said you messed everything up," I say quietly. "You didn't mess everything up. I just climbed to the top of an ancient stone wall," I hesitate a second. "Do you know what that *means?*"

He smiles. "No, but I'm pretty sure you're going to tell me. You always do."

"Hey! I'm complimenting you, be careful." I say. "It means that I can do that. I can do physical stuff I never thought I could. Because it turns out it's all about attitude. I was down on myself. I wasn't able to do things with Alyssa and Jenna because I didn't believe I had it in me. You've shown me I do. You've given me a second chance with my girls, Gene. I'm so grateful."

"You're welcome. I knew you had it in you, you know. I'm sorry I called you vain. You're not," he answers, squeezing my hand. "You've one of the spunkiest, funniest, brightest women I've ever met, and you scale a wall like, well, like an amateur, but you did it! And if you like to look at yourself in the mirror now and then, that's okay with me."

"Okay with you? I'm glad I have your permission, Sir." I chuckle. I love taking the piss out of him! Usually, he'd retort with a dig, but his face looks rather serious now.

"I didn't mean it like that, Katherine. I…" He exhales deeply, then continues, "I'm sorry I've made such a mess of everything for so long, but hopefully, I can get us out of here, change your past, and help you find happiness," He's not looking at me, he's staring out into the Valley, over vast stretches of green vineyards. The sun has started to set. Bright orange clouds fall behind the grey-walled village below us. The sky is lilac coloured and serene. Scenes in the old village play out for us like a silent movie. This place from where we watch that movie feels like ours, and ours alone.

As I put my head on his shoulder, I daydream about how I'm going to try tossing a football with the girls when we finally get home.

"Happiness?" I whisper. "I think I'm already on my way."

I snuggle in closer to him. He's got one knee curled up into his body, and the other is dangling over the edge of the wall. I'm not afraid I'll lose my balance sitting here, because he's got a firm grip on me at my waist. I don't want to climb down yet. I don't want to go.

"Let's not go yet." He pulls me in closer, reading my mind.

"What?"

"I'd love to just sit here with you tonight. Watch the world below us, like—"

"Like a play? And we're in the box seats up above?"

"Exactly." He grins. "Exactly. Look!"

I peer down to where he's pointing, and see a black and white border collie, hopping along on three legs.

"Poor fella," I say.

The dog must be arthritic, too, because even his hopping is slow and methodical. His owner is a tall, slender man who walks with his head held high, shoulders back. It looks like he's been formally trained in marching, and yet, his pace is purposefully as slow, if not slower, than the dog. He lets his dog go ahead of him, perhaps to give the old canine some sense of control of his ailing body.

"Gosh, now that's what you'd call a dog on its last legs," I say, and hope Gene laughs. He does. We keep watching the man and his best friend, silently praying the dog will get to their car soon, because it's almost painful to watch. When they finally reach the car, the man opens the back hatch, bends down and gently picks up his dog. He gives him a tender kiss between the eyes, then places him inside.

"Aw," we say in unison.

Our attention is soon distracted by the loud haste of a man and woman coming out of a grey stone building. The man is carrying so many gift boxes and shopping bags, he cannot see where he's going. The woman is hustling toward their car, keys in hand, wearing high heels and a white, form-fitting dress.

"Hey! She's not carrying a thing! Not a thing! Now, is that really fair?" Gene asks.

I give the scene another once-over. "No, she's a total bitch," I laugh. "See how she's walking way ahead of him? She's not even acknowledging him. I wonder if they're married."

"Oh, they're not married. He's trying to impress her. He hasn't known her long. If he's smart, soon enough, he won't take that shit. He'll tell her to buy less, and carry more."

"Gene!" I'm not at all incredulous, though, and when I catch him looking my way, we both crack up.

A small boy is running along a riverbank. A man walks behind him, trying to keep up.

Gene is pensive. I wonder if he's thinking about his son.

"Logan was nine, like your son," I say. "If we can save Logan, maybe it will feel a little like, well, like you're saving your own son," I immediately regret it the minute the words leave my lips.

"Maybe." He surprises me. "Maybe. I don't really know, but if I can help you, I'm just one person shy of being free, and getting back to him. So, maybe."

We sit in silence again, staring out into the vast, dark space before us, but he squeezes my hand. I start to shake a little; the wind is causing a chill. He moves his hand from my waist to my arm, and pulls me in closer, rubbing my arm and thighs up and down to warm me.

"See that tower over there?" He points to a large, round stone tower just steps away from us – but accessible to us only by crossing the top of this wall. "We could get inside that tower from here. It would be warmer for you there; the walls would break the wind. We should check it out! I'll be right behind you."

I don't even need to think this over. There is no way I'm: a) falling off a high stone wall and b) forcing him to watch my fat ass jiggling in front of

him as I pull myself along the ledge. I can't bear to do that.

"I'm fat. You won't like having my fat ass in your face."

"Jesus, Katherine, I… I care about you. I don't care one ninth letter of the Greek alphabet about the shape of your body. I care about the shape of your heart and mind, but if you must know, I think you're very sexy just the way you are."

"You do?" I need to hear that again. "Er, and what's the ninth letter of the Greek alphabet?"

"I do. And it's iota. Which is also a noun meaning tiny amount," he says and gives me a kiss on the lips. "I wish you'd believe that you're beautiful. Maybe you need more time around the right kind of man. But trust me, you're beautiful."

I should take a leap of faith here. I really do want to check out that tower. "Okay, but you go first. I need to follow your lead."

He starts inching out ahead of me, his legs straddling the wall, his torso moving little by little, to reach the tower. I follow what he's doing, and begin inching, bit by bit, pushing my hands and legs against the wall to move my torso slowly along the ledge.

When I finally reach him, he's already standing inside, looking out the tower window. He puts out his arms for me, and I let him lift me up and inside. His arms are strong around me; I feel so light. I forget all about my weight when I'm in his embrace.

The tower is beautiful: a rounded stone walled room, with two windows overlooking Rhone Valley. I stare out the window and wonder how much of Provence we'd actually be able to see on a clear, sunlit day. As dusk turns to dark, all I can see are fields of grape vines, and hundreds of stars. The sky is a black velvet blanket, painted with fine, sparkling crystal.

"It seems a shame to waste this stunning view on a night like this." He smiles, pulls me into his chest, and hugs me tight. "Katherine," he whispers as he kisses the top of my hair, "I want you, and I want to do it better this time."

"I thought we earned an A for effort the first time," I smile up at him, but I'm quietly hoping we last longer this time. I could make love to him for hours.

Gene lifts my t-shirt over my head as I raise my arms. As soon as our shoes and clothing are out of the way, his mouth finds my breasts. He licks each one gently, in a circular motion, taking his time. *Groan*. He's only licking and sucking my nipples, and I'm already aroused. He kisses his way down my body, falling to his knees, and slowly, almost too slowly, takes off my panties. I step out quickly, finding my balance by pressing down on his shoulders.

"Oh my God, look at you!" he says, stroking my hips and putting his lips against my tummy. He caresses my legs, all the way down to my ankles, then up my sides, to my breasts again. Soon, his mouth

meets mine. It's a long, hard kiss, yet, I am insatiable. I want more. I pull away and walk backward to the closest wall. My knees are starting to feel weak; the anticipation electrifies me. He follows slowly on his knees, crawling on the straw-covered ground. Chuckling, he gives me a lustful grin and keeps crawling toward me. When he finally reaches me, he gently grasps my thighs, and slowly licks each side, up and down, up and down. I throw my head back and become uncharacteristically quiet; just a few moans and pounds of my hand against the stone wall.

I'm lost in sensation; so lost, I'm not even sure if the moans are coming from me or him. After a long while, he looks up at me with desire in his eyes. His boxers come off, and he stands up.

I grip the stone wall at the window frame with my left hand, and his shoulder with my right, steadying myself as we become lost in one another. I close my eyes but can still see him, feel him, every delicious part of him.

It's almost too much; I'm afraid I'll break. I start to make a move, but before I need to say anything, he's on his back on the straw-covered ground, holding my hands, beckoning me to join him down there.

I fall forward and start kissing his neck, his lips, his chest, his nipples. My hair brushes his face, but he smiles at me, unbothered. He touches everything that feels good, ever so gently, as if he's known me a thousand years. Our eyes lock before he puts his hands on my shoulders and rolls me over.

I hold on tight, wrapping my legs around him, our bodies rocking as one. I can feel myself losing it. I want this to last for hours, but it can't, won't. The excitement in me is about to explode, sending shivers from the bottom of my spine to all the pleasure points in my body. *He's hitting my g-spot, my f-spot and my every letter of the alphabet-spot!*

Swear words clamour in my head, but I say nothing; I just gasp and try to get enough breath to keep up with him. It's just the two of us and nothing else. I forget our problems and the rest of the world for these few searing moments of ecstasy.

When he calls my name it shoots right through me. I quiver, all my body trembling with joy and pleasure. *Oh my God, who do I thank?*

He collapses on top of me, breathless, and I gasp, tears in my eyes as he sweeps a strand of damp hair off my face.

"You drive me crazy at times," he whispers, kissing my eyebrows, nose, and lips, "but I love you."

"Same here for the crazy part. We do crazy well, and I love you, too," I blink, the perspiration stinging my eyes, but I must look at him, into him, and remember every precious detail of this. I want to thank him a million times, and I hope he sees that in my face.

Our eyes stay locked for several moments, while

our heartbeats slow their march to a soothing pace, and we finally surrender to fatigue. He looks around and grabs a torn, but clean-looking blanket from under the far window, picks off a few pieces of straw, then covers us up entirely, and lies down on his back. I put my head on his chest, match my breathing with his, and snuggle in for a peaceful sleep. We breathe in unison, and there's no other sound. Nothing seems to matter except us, together, always. We say nothing else, there's no need. I can't remember who falls asleep first.

———

WHEN WE AWAKEN, it's light outside… and I'm pretty sure we're not in Mornas anymore.

14

I'M NOT LYING ON STRAW-COVERED GROUND ANYMORE. I'm lying on cement.

Gene must have dressed me, because despite this cold slab beneath me, I'm not shivering. I'm back in shoes, panties and the big Bon Jovi T shirt I grabbed and threw on after we made love for the first time, and stormed out – 'It's My Life' scrawled across it.

I sit up and look around. Yellow lines, parked cars. We're in a parking lot, or maybe a drive-in.

"We can't be here, we might be seen." Gene is standing over me. He's dressed in his white dress shirt and tuxedo pants. They're torn from the wall climb, and covered in dirt.

"Seen? Who will see us? The aliens? Is it that bad?" I'm half joking, but when I see his deadpan face, my heart starts beating even faster than it already was. Where the hell are we now?

"No, we're still on Earth, sweetheart, but it's another time. It's 1993. Or, it had better be, or someone's finally going to fire me. Not that I'd mind that much. I guess we'll find out soon enough."

"How did we get here so fast?"

"I heard people walking up the tower stairs this morning, so I quickly brought us here. I used my wish, to be safe."

"What? No bumpy ride this time?"

He laughs. "No, and honestly, I have no clue as to why. I haven't figured out how to make it more or less bumpy. Maybe it was easier this time because it was me doing the wishing? I'm amazed you slept through it."

I stand up and take a look around. We're definitely in a parking lot, but luckily, no one seems to be around. It looks to be mid-afternoon, from the way the sun is sitting in the sky.

After walking the path a while, I recognize this park. I remember it wasn't very popular with my teenage friends because it had a play structure for preschoolers. It's also far from our school and my house. I let out a deep sigh. Gene leads me to a park bench, gestures for me to take a seat, then sits beside me.

He tucks a loose hair behind my ear, then leans over, and kisses me gently. God, that feels good.

"Are you okay, Katherine? I know this is a lot to take in."

"I'm fine. I'm getting used to this with you. So, you've used your wish, and this is my wish number two, huh. Do you think we can do it? We can change history?"

"I honestly didn't think it was allowed Katherine, and yet, the magic wouldn't have taken us here if we weren't supposed to come. I think we need to figure out where your friends are right now, and try to stop that accident. But there are no guarantees. You need to know that."

"We could go to my house and see what day and time it is. Then we could head to Murphy's lookout point from there," I say, not really sure of what I'm saying at all.

"Or find a way to stop the drag race from ever taking place," Gene suggests. "But what about your Gram? She'll be home."

"Oh no. Right. We'll have to distract her. Do you think you can help with that? She's never seen you in this time. You could talk to her like a... like a guy selling vacuums or something, while I try to find out where Ben is?"

His eyes sparkle and crinkle upward with his amused grin. "Do you really remember people selling vacuums door to door in your high school years? Since when did you go to high school in the 1940s?"

I take my hand away from his, feeling the need to defend myself. "Listen, Mr. Ingenious, I'm new at this, and I'm nervous. I'm sorry if the plot isn't panning out like 'Back to the Future', okay? Give it time."

I can feel my entire body panicking as I speak. How the hell am I going to avoid my grandmother and Ben and everyone else, because I look so much older I'll freak them out, but still change history and save two lives?

I have no idea how to save someone from dying in another time. I hardly know how to iron a blouse properly, or cook the girls' dinner without burning it; this seems somewhat more challenging. And how am I supposed to accomplish what I have to in one day, when we don't even have a car?

The moment I ask the question in my mind, a white stretch limo pulls up to the curb. That's just uncanny. But then again, I'm sitting here on a park bench with a genie who has become my lover, and it's 1993 again. Nothing should surprise me anymore, and yet, I'm surprised.

This has *got* to stop happening so often, or I'm going to pee my pants all the way through. Vaginal childbirth twice over is no friend to sneezing fits or being freaked out by genie magic.

Gene takes my hand again and leads me toward the car. "This is our ride." He opens the back door and lets me get in, then slides in beside me.

The driver pulls away from the curb. Oh yes, this is going to be inconspicuous around town. A white stretch limo. Me, 20 years older, and a genie in... what the heck is he wearing again anyway? I take another look.

Oh no, we're definitely going to have to change our clothes. Gene's in those torn pants, and my shirt mentions a song that wasn't released until 2000.

He reads my mind. "Here, let me see what I can do about this, without actually wishing," Gene closes his eyes tight, clenching his fists. I look down at my shirt and realize it's now an Elmo t-shirt and matching red leggings.

"Gene! I'm not in preschool!"

"Uh, sorry, I can get this, just give me a minute. I got you the limo! I can do this!"

I look down again, and I'm in a limo driver's black uniform, complete with hat and visor.

"This isn't working." I notice I'm back in my Bon Jovi shirt. He's still in the tux.

He opens his eyes, but doesn't look at me. He looks down and says nothing.

I guess it's time to go home, raid my old closet for oversized shirts and pants and hope for the best.

THE SMALL HOUSE where I grew up isn't far from my high school. It's on a street lined with majestic oak trees. As we drive up Penton Way towards Davis Place, I notice the architecture of the homes for the first time. I wasn't especially interested in columns and patios and awnings when I was a teenager. Now I notice the homes are mostly bungalows, built in the 1960s, but some have new additions. Ours never had a new anything. After my parents died, Gram put all the insurance money into taking care of me and my sister. Maybe a little gambling and whiskey, too; let's be honest, I adore the woman, but her Twitter handle isn't @AngelicAssGrandma.

"Oh, crap. My sister. Cici. We're probably going to run into her, too. How in hell is this not going to be a time travel disaster?"

Cici now lives five streets over and has three children of her own, but if memory serves, we are about to find her at home, sharing a room with yours truly. A very messy, disorganized room – hard to believe given that she is now the Queen of the Label Machine – at her house and, sometimes, at mine.

We park just steps away from where I grew up. "Gene… Are you sure we can do this?" I get out of the car with him.

"Well, we may have a friend on our side now. Look, your Gram's in the window, jumping up and down in a bright orange jogging suit and headband. See?"

I crouch down behind a bush beside the house so she doesn't see me, and peek in the window. There's my Gram, being my Gram. She's a vision in '90s neon, jumping up and down to loud music coming from the speakers in the corner of the room. When I put my ear in closer, I can catch her shouting the lyrics to the song:

"Whoot, there it is! *Whoot, there it is!*"

Hands on hips, pelvis forward, she jumps forward, then backward, then pelvis forward again, working her *gludimus maximus*, as she has always, to my great amusement, incorrectly called it.

"She's entertaining, that's for sure," Gene whispers in my ear. "Okay, so we've got this limo. Let's be producers. Let's sell her the idea of Reality Television. She's a hoot, and so ahead of her time. I'll talk to her as if we want to sign her to a show, and at the same time, do some detective work. Find out where you are, and if you've given Ben the money yet. And I guess we need to find us some clothes." He whispers the last part, and I know he wishes he could be more consistent with his magic.

"Where I am? *Oh* Right. Young me. Okay, so I have to stay here? No. I really don't want to!" I start to pout. He looks up at the window again, tells me to *shhh* and pushes me down to the ground so I won't be seen. I'm pleased he is finally thinking things through, but I wish I could talk to my sister and my Gram. I'm starting to feel homesick, which is weird, because I am, in fact, home. But I miss my own house, and my dear girls, and I'd really love to talk to my Gram right now.

"Petal, I think it's probably for the best."

"No, no, I don't want to!" I resist.

Just as he reaches down to take my hand and lead me back to the limo, from out of nowhere, Gram comes up behind him and hits him on the head with a red brick.

"*Take that, you vile creature!*" cries the vision in '90s neon. Gene falls straight down like a tower to the ground, probably suffering a second concussion when he hits it. At least his head has fallen on the grass, not the cement pathway. I kneel down to him and put my ear to his mouth. He's breathing, but rapidly, and his eyes aren't open.

"Holy shit, Gram, er, woman! You've knocked him out cold!"

"Yea. I may be old, but I see everything. I saw you two standing at my window. I saw you crouching in the bush, telling him no. Dimwit won't hurt you again, dearie." She throws the brick behind the bush, gives Gene a little kick to make sure he doesn't move (he doesn't), and takes my hand to lead me into the house. Then she does a double-take, and her face turns white. She stops in her tracks and just stares at me.

"Molly?"

Molly was my mother. I'm not sure why she recognizes me as her. Oh God, I must look like my mother did back then, before she passed away. Isn't that something? Now what the hell am I going to do? Tell her I'm from the future? No. No. *Fuckity!* This situation would definitely piss off Doc Brown.

"No, no, I'm not her."

"Molly dear, you've come back to haunt me! *Hallelujah!* I knew you would!" she laughs and claps her hands, then leaps forward and gives me the tightest hug she has ever given me.

"Mooooooan. The woman doesn't give up does she?" Gene is coming to. Oh, this poor man's strength and persistence, beaten to a pulp by the same old woman in a matter of days!

Gram looks down and pulls away from our hug. "Quick, Molly, into the house, we'll be safe from him there." She starts to pull me toward the house, then stops and laughs at herself, "For cryin' out loud, I'm so forgetful sometimes, you could probably just fly through the wall couldn't ya. Well at least I'm getting out of here. I'll go call the police…"

"Gram… *Mom!*" I pull her back to me. By now I realize resisting any of this is futile, but I can at least try to avoid cops locking up Gene in another time. "He's fine. He's my partner. Come on."

"Partner? What do you mean? And, I know everyone's trying to be fashion forward these days, but why are you two dressed like hooligans?" She looks confused. I decide to leave it unexplained, for now.

"Can we please just go inside?"

She lets go of my hand, walks to the open front door and motions for me to follow. By now, Gene is standing up behind me, but he's not talking to me.

He's muttering under his breath. Words I probably don't want to hear.

———

ONCE INSIDE, Gram heads to the kitchen next door and calls out to me, "You don't want me to call anyone, I guess that's because you're not actually here, right?" I can hear her chuckling. "Do ghosts drink tea?"

I don't answer right away. I push Gene down on the living room sofa, and stare at him firmly, whispering, "Don't say anything!" His eyebrows furrow, and he starts to sulk. "You have a flashlight?" I call to Gram. She takes a small one from the drawer in the desk beside her and hands it to me. I flash it into his eyes.

"*Ow*! Now you? What are you women trying to do to me!" he shouts.

"Hang on, I'm checking to make sure you don't have a concussion."

"She nailed me with a brick at the back of the head. What do you think?" he barks at me.

"You two know each other? Well why didn't you tell me?" Gram is quiet a minute as she thinks about that. "Oh! Oh no. No no no. I don't want him in my house. I'm not ready." Gram starts pacing back and forth across the pink carpet.

I stand up and deal with Gene first. "You're fine. You have lots of other problems, but no concussion."

"Funny," he replies, still sulking, crossing his arms and not budging from the sofa.

I turn to face Gram. "Yes, we know each other," I start to say, but she interrupts.

"I knew it. He's the Grim Reaper. It's finally my day. And he brought you with him to make my entry into the next world a little less frightening, is that it, Molly?"

I have no idea how to answer her. She doesn't give me time. She grabs the flashlight from my hand and slams it down on the desk.

"Well I'll have none of it. None. Of. It. Begone, Dark One!" she points at Gene dramatically, then points to the door. "I've got plenty of life in me yet, and three more songs on that *Hot Hits* CD that I gotta groove to."

Gene uses Gram's dramatic exit demands to get up and mime from behind her. He's rather pathetic at charades. I'll have to remember this if we're ever partnered in a game. I think he's trying to tell me he's going to go search Gram's and my closets for clothes for us, but he could be asking me if I want a cappuccino? I nod briefly, and keep improvising.

"Ma'am," I say, taking her arm gently and leading her back to the sofa. "I'm no ghost, and he's not the Grim Reaper. I suppose I look like someone you know, but we're actually TV producers. We want to tell you about something called Reality TV."

"Reality TV? Is that a booster shot? I got all my shots. Don't need more."

"No, no, it's a kind of television that we're on the verge of inventing," I say. I wonder just how much I'm messing with the space-time-continuum here. Can I make it so 'Keeping Up With The Kardashians' never airs?

"So, you want me to audition for it? It's not 'The Dating Game' is it? I hate that show. I lost my husband years ago. Don't need no man. I'm happy like this." She folds her arms. She looks annoyed. I have no idea how to make this work, but keep winging it.

"Yes, well, it's not the 'Dating Game'. It would be a show all about you. About your life. We're also interested in, er, your granddaughters. Can you tell us where they are right now?"

"Like a documentary? Aren't those as boring as cold porridge? Hey, wait. Is this about how their parents died? I don't wanna drag those girls through that again. I won't." She stands up, hands on hips.

"That's great you're so protective, Gram, er, Grandma. We should call the show 'Grandma'."

"No thanks. I ain't no Grandma. More like a Badass Grandma, and I don't think I want you in my home anymore, Molly-look-alike. I figure you just want my vote, or my money, and besides that, you're creeping me out." She walks toward me, and I just want to hug her and tell her that everything is really fine, and she's been such a comfort to me all these years, such a confidante, but then I see Gene, holding a bag full of clothes, rushing out the door and back into the limo. Gram hears the door slam, but doesn't see him. When she turns to look out the window, he's already inside the car.

"Now, where is Handsome going so fast?"

"We have another appointment. That's Hollywood for you. Busy, busy, busy!" I try to laugh it off.

She eyes me up and down, and then holds out her hand rather graciously.

"Thanks for thinking of our family," she says, letting go of my hand after a firm shake, "but I ain't signing nothing, and especially nothing about our reality. Our reality has been harsh, but we're getting by now. I don't want those girls' names dragged through the mud. They're special girls. And so beautiful…" she trails off, her thoughts drifting. "You should have seen them last night, before Cat's big grad dance, just glowing. Got lots of pictures of them together, and me too. Cici and Cat are out dropping off the film for developing now."

"Oh yeah? Right now huh?" I try to sound casual, but need to find out where 'young me' has gone. I vaguely remember that first day of summer vacation, starting with waking up under the stars beside Ben.

What had I done between him driving me home and picking me up again for the race? I couldn't remember.

"That, and my clever Cat is keen to get some job experience this summer. She's going to college in the fall, and we need the money, so Cici is helping her hand out resumes at the places where she's worked before. Typing, filing, that kind of stuff. They may end up working together, which should be interesting, since all they usually do in that shared room of theirs is argue." Gram chuckles, and then I notice her lower her gaze, and her protective wall goes up. "I'm going on and on and you have places to be. This won't be on your reality show now will it? You can't do that, can you?"

"Gosh, no!" I say, patting her on the back as I leave the house. "Thanks for all your help. I really wish you all the best," I say.

"Thanks, Molly," she says with a wink, as I get into the limo. "Thanks for the visit, dear."

"You're welcome." I decide not to argue, but hope that she doesn't go around telling all her friends that her daughter's ghost came by in a limousine today.

As soon as I slide in, I turn to Gene, who's finally made his genie magic work, and is wearing a pair of jeans, a Beastie Boys t-shirt, and a Blue Jays' ball cap.

"I haven't gone with Ben to the race yet. There's still time to stop him from racing. Quick. We have to go to his place," I take off his cap, "but not wearing this. Never wear this." I laugh, and start rummaging through the bag of clothes at his feet, hoping to find something to wear.

"What? What makes you think I haven't lived in this year before? Huh? I've been around, girlfriend."

"That. Don't say that either." I chuckle. "You can't pull it off."

"The Blue Jays are going to win the World Series, against the Phillies. This is the *perfect* cap to wear. The fans are gearing up," he says.

"Okay, fine, but then I'm wearing this," I say, pulling out some white Keds sneakers, a large white t-shirt, and some worn overalls. "What do you think of that?" I grin.

"I think you're going to regret those overalls in a few hours, but at least they aren't Mom Jeans." He grins.

"I love Mom Jeans!" I laugh. "What's wrong with Mom Jeans?"

Gene leans over and kisses me hard on the mouth. "Nothing, so long as you're in them."

"Smooth. But so predictable." I smile. "Okay, let's go find Ben."

As the limo pulls away from my childhood home, a large part of me wants to stay behind. I turn to look through the window, watching the house get smaller and smaller. "Bye, old house," I say quietly. "Be good to us while I'm gone."

15

BEN'S HOUSE ISN'T FAR FROM MY OLD STREET, AND along the way, I see my primary school – the same one my girls attended. It looks newly built, and of course, it has been, and I smile when I recognize the Book Mobile parked beside it. That trailer was parked beside my school for a number of years before our local library was built. It was my favourite hideaway as a kid.

I remember the effort it took my small legs to climb up the steep, rubber-matted stairs on that trailer. I always felt a surge of joy when I reached the top and discovered the door open with the librarian seated at a small desk inside. Somehow, it felt so different from a regular library. It was small, dark, and smelled of brand new books. I liked how Gram let me ride my bike there on my own, and how only a few people were ever inside, reading books on the floor along with me. Sometimes, I was in that mobile library all alone; just me, and those lovely books. It felt like I'd discovered my own secret cave.

As we arrive closer to Ben's street, I ask the driver to stop. I don't want Ben to notice our limousine, or me. We'll have to figure out how we're going to talk to him about the race later. We just need to find him first, but it's starting to get darker out. We're running out of time.

Gene opens my door, and I get out and start walking toward Ben's home. There it is: the split-level house just three doors down. Ben's on the driveway! He's washing his Mustang. Of course. He would do that. Not so much to make it sparkle for the race; he's thinking about his strategy. I remember he told me he likes to think things through when he's washing his car. That makes sense; I do my best thinking in the shower. It must be that water helps creativity.

There's a large oak tree up ahead, so I pull Gene behind it. "We don't want to be seen by anyone," I whisper. Gene smirks, pushes me against the wide oak, and slips his hands down the back of my overalls.

"I'm starting to see why these overalls were a hit among teens." He laughs, and draws me in for a long, lingering kiss.

"Gene," I pull back, "This is delicious, and I feel like a teenager again, dressed like this, but we have serious business to attend to!" I pull away. As I peer around the tree to catch a glimpse of Ben again, everything I ever thought I knew about him, about us, comes crashing down like an old building being demolished. Fast and furious.

Ben's leaning against his Mustang, the one I loaned him money for, so he could buy it. He has a sponge in one hand, and the other hand wrapped around a girl's waist. I would recognize her anywhere. Cathy Hollows is leaning against him. Kissing him. *He's kissing her back.*

I feel heat rising in my cheeks, and turn away, burying my face in Gene's chest. How could Ben do this to me? To us? I thought he was sincere about how he felt about me? That he was okay to wait? Were those all lies? I start sobbing; making little whining noises as I cry. Gene tries to calm me, at first with just his eyes, then, covering my mouth softly so I won't be heard. I'm still crying hard, unable to catch my breath, when he physically turns me around to see what's happening.

Ben has pushed Cathy off of him, and he's talking to her. He's got a very serious look on his face. She's wearing short jean shorts, and tries to play legsie with him, curling up to him, her naked leg wrapped around his knee as she looks up to his face and responds to him. He doesn't move her leg away, but he doesn't look happy about their conversation either.

I've never felt more torn in my life. I want to rush over there and confront him; to remind him of our powerful love, but I remember I look like my Mom, in Keds and overalls. I'll freak both of them out.

Ben throws the sponge into the pail on the driveway, grabs his leather jacket on the front steps, and pulls out his car keys. That's it Ben, walk away. You don't need her. You just need us.

Then he bends down and gives her a kiss, on the lips. *On the lips. A kiss. My Ben.*

I want to scream. I wonder if I scream loud enough, he'll come to me, recognize me... believe my story. I know it can't happen. Gene is holding me back. He pulls me toward the limo.

"Come on, we have to get out of here before he drives past us," he whispers.

"He's scum. He's actually scum," I wipe away tears.

"I wouldn't say scum, Petal," he helps me slide in to the backseat and tells the driver to pull away fast. "He's a misguided teenage boy. He's making a mistake," he says as he wipes some of the wetness off my face with his t-shirt. "I wish I'd had the chance to date you years ago, instead of now, when I'm trapped in my life. When I may not get the chance to stay with you... and I don't know how I'll get back to you..." he trails off, realizing he's only going to make me cry more.

Perhaps trying to help stop me crying, the driver turns on the radio as our limo pulls off of Ben's street. It's the Annie Lennox hit, *Little Bird*, about a woman

who wishes she could just become a bird, and fly away from all her rage and fear.

Tears are streaming down my face now. I turn the song down and turn to Gene. He just looks at me, kisses my forehead, and pulls me in close.

"Driver, can you stop for a while? We just need to stop a while."

I rest my head on Gene's shoulder, close my eyes, and do something I haven't done in years. I pray.

WHEN OUR CAR pulls up to the starting line, other cars are already ahead of us. My former peers are gathered behind Jake and Ben's cars, standing on the hoods of their own cars, waving sparklers in the air. "Stay here, please, it's safer, for both of us," I tell Gene.

I get out of the car, slam the door, and stand behind some other girl at the side of the road. When she steps down into the ditch, I look at her more closely from behind, and realize it's me. Weird. So, so weird. I'm getting goose bumps. I try not to think about it too long. My brain may explode.

I stay on the side of the road, but rush farther ahead so she won't recognize me. I'm not going to step down into that ditch and do nothing – not this time. This time, I'm taking action. I don't want Logan or Ben to die. Even if Ben is interested in Cathy, and I never saw it; that doesn't matter. I don't want him to die.

"Okay, people." Cathy walks to the space between Ben's and Jake's cars and pulls out a small plastic Canadian flag from her inside jean-jacket pocket. Before she can say, "Let's have a race to remember!" I start running ahead, and then use all I've got to turn the run into a sprint. If I can just get to the point where the boys' cars swerved into each other briefly, I can make it so Ben avoids hitting Logan on the road up ahead, because they'll have to stop. They'll have to stop for me.

I can hear hooting and hollering, and it starts to spit rain. *Weeeaaaaaaaaa.* A siren. It's the police sirens. God. They can't stop it. I know that now. It's all up to me. I can do this. I need to do this.

I look behind me and realize the cars are closing in on me. I've missed the first minor collision. Damnit! Now I have to find that dog.

I look down at my racing feet, willing them to move faster. Someone runs up beside me, to my right. It's blurry because I'm running so fast. Baseball cap. Large feet. Neon sneakers. Gene. Gene came anyway.

"Katherine, stop. You aren't doing this," he shouts. "It's nuts."

"It's what has to be done to save lives, Gene," I say, and stop in my tracks. We're nearly at the top of the point. I turn to scan the ditch and field to my left, and see a large black shadow moving fast toward us.

Oh God. No. No!

Gene has run into the field to find little Logan. But I still need to stop that dog, or Ben will slam on his breaks and crash through the windshield.

The dog sees me, and thinks it's a game of tag. He darts into the road faster than last time, crosses to the right side, then cocks his head at me at the left side, like he's asking me to make the next move. *God, think fast, what is my next move?* I can't think. I simply lunge forward at him, hoping to chase him out of the road.

I don't feel the pain of being hit by Jake's car, but I instantly know it's happened. It's a hard, heavy hit to my head, but as I fall, I can still see and hear people around me: Ben's car swerving to the far left to miss me and the dog, driving backwards into the ditch. Jake, slowly stepping out of his car, a bloody gash on his forehead, looking dazed and confused, but alive. Gene, holding a frightened but safe Logan in his arms, placing him down in the field, running toward me, screaming.

I'm lying on my back, trying to focus on Gene's face. He's holding my hand and talking to me, but I can barely see his features now. It hurts to keep my eyes open. It hurts to try to talk. I want to stop breathing. I want to stop trying.

"Katherine, you're badly hurt. You need to wish yourself back to 2013, back to health in 2013," Gene is telling me, over and over, touching my face, kissing my cheek.

"But. Last. Wish. Yours," I try to explain. "You. I wanted." I can hardly breathe now.

"Katherine, shhh. Save your energy. You wanted to set me free, I know, I want that too, more than you'll ever know." He kisses my lips gently. I can feel his tears on my lips. I don't think I've ever felt his tears before. I don't want to lose him. If I wish myself back to health, I'll lose him.

"You have to use the last wish Katherine. I can come back to you. Someday, I'll find a way, and get back to you, to us. But you're no good to me dead," Gene whispers at my ear, and takes my hand. "Petal. People are gathering, starting to wonder what this is all about. An ambulance will be here soon. You'd better make it quick."

I want to free him. I want to use that last wish to make a life for us! I want to argue with him; to scream from the depths of my soul into the cold, wet air, but I've lost my will. I can barely speak. I just want to go to sleep. I open my eyes to look into his beautiful green ones, one last time.

"Gene," I whisper, squeezing his hands. "Goodbye. Thank you. Thanks for every…" He puts a finger to my lips, and I know he understands.

One deep, strong breath, to get me through this. "I wish to return to 2013, healthy and happy," I say, tears streaming down my face.

I close my eyes and hope I don't wake up in a nightmare.

16

THE FIRST THING I NOTICE WHEN I REGAIN consciousness is the smell. It's that scent I detest so strongly: Eau de Hospital smell; the reek of sickness and Savlon. I don't want to be here. I open my eyes, searching the room for someone, anyone, familiar. Get me out of here! Get me out!

No one is here to help me. Where's that little button? I thought there was a panic button on all beds in all hospitals. Now I'm in a panic, because I can't press panic!

I start to feel hot, and begin thrashing around in the bed. As I try to sit up, the sudden pain in my chest area is excruciating. I lay back down and let my head fall back on my pillow, but I keep my eyes open. Wait. Someone is here!

"Gram." I smile up at her beautiful, wrinkled, worried face. "Gram."

"Go and have a heart attack on me, huh, cupcake? Way to treat an old lady. I'm supposed to croak first, you got that? Me! You got it all wrong!"

As she talks, a nurse comes in, takes my hand, and shows me the remote at the side of my bed. She presses a button, and I slowly start to rise up to a comfortable sitting position. She places a pillow behind my lower back. "Is that good, Katherine?"

She called me Katherine. Oh God, I miss Gene. Where is he? Did he make it back with me?

"It's fine, thanks," I mutter and turn back to Gram, who has taken my hand. "Gram. Where's Gene? Is he back at the house? Still sleeping in the basement?"

"Basement? Honey, you're in a condo. I don't know what you're talkin' about." She bends to whisper at my ear, "Keep pressing that little button, I think the morphine's relaxing you."

Condo? What is she going on about? I couldn't afford to own a condo, and all those condo fees, on my salary. Something isn't right here. I look down at my hips and tummy. They're practically non-existent.

"Oh my God Gram! I've lost so much weight!"

"Well yes, three days of steady hospital diet will do that…" she trails off. She's standing by my window, reading all my Get-Well cards.

I frantically look around the room for anything with a date on it. If I've lost the weight, and I live in a condo, maybe Gene accidentally sent me to the future

again. Gram looks the same, though. Although, she looks a little more made up than usual, and she isn't carrying a cane/genie beating weapon. Is that a designer purse she's carrying? Okay, that's just weird.

There's a small TV remote at my side table. I grab it and switch on the TV, but not before one deep intake of breath, to brace myself for whatever this new reality brings.

"Better not be tunin' in to my show, cupcake, you know I'm pissed at them producers for airing that last episode. Let an old lady play strip poker in privacy."

Her show? Producers? The poker part isn't that much of a shock, but still, what planet did Gene send me to?

I don't get any answers, because a tall, dark-haired male nurse comes bustling into the room and heads toward Gram, just as the midday newscast comes on. "I know you must get this all the time," he says, and then he giggles, and covers up his mouth. "My boyfriend and I just love all you have to say in support of gay marriage. We think you're amazing! Would you sign this for me?" He pulls off his nursing scrubs to reveal a cartoonlike version of Gram, front and centre, on his t-shirt. Above the cartoon is the title: Badass Grandma: MTV. Weeknights @ 9 EST. Gram takes the Sharpie from the nurse's hand and scribbles her illegible autograph across her own image. She smiles.

"No problem. I'm getting used to signing behinds

in boxers, so this is a welcome change. Hope you two get married. Good luck to yous."

I need ice chips. A mountain of ice chips. I can't believe any of this. I grab a cup, toss it back in desperation, and the ice chips fall across my face and down to the ground. Gram comes to my aid, picking up the ice chips that have fallen across my blanket.

"You're sick of the fame. I know. I know, dearie. I hope the stress of it all didn't cause…" She looks at me with those knowing blue eyes, and I have to interrupt, though I really don't know what put me in this bed.

"Oh no, Gram, I'm sure it wasn't that. It was my lifestyle."

"Yes, running that gym of yours was too much for one woman. I hope when you go back to work, you hire an Assistant Manager."

"Right," I say, trying to digest what she's telling me. I'm about to ask her more about my career, when the newscaster mentions a name I recognize. It startles me, so I have to look up, and turn up the sound.

"Logan Brown has announced he's running for Leader of Canada's Liberal Party in the fall election. Brown, a 28-year-old lawyer with the firm, Morgan & Cameron in Ottawa, was the youngest Canadian to become an MP. He's been outspoken about his platform, and is looking to make changes to several existing laws, including laws regarding underage drinking and driving, and speeding."

I drop the remote in my lap and start sobbing. It's not like when I was sobbing in the candy section of Walmart: that was shame, guilt, and remorse. That was different. I'm different. Now I'm sobbing with great, heaving sighs of relief.

It's over. I didn't cause anyone's death; in fact, everything seems a whole lot brighter in this new life. Gram starts rubbing my back, then puts her cheek to mine.

"I know, dear, it stirs the soul, doesn't it? You cry every time you see him on the news, but I won't tell anyone. You deserve to let the tears flow. If you hadn't pushed Logan out of the way of that silly boy's car, he wouldn't be alive and doing the wonderful work he's doing today. You ended up with a broken heart that summer. But you saved a little boy's life."

"Broken heart?" I say, half-hearing her. I pushed Logan out of the way? That's what everyone thinks? I suppose no one saw Gene after he carried Logan to safety, but I saw him. He carried that boy like he was carrying his own little boy; his face dark and intense, his body geared up to do whatever he had to do to save both of us. Everyone assumed I was the heroine of the story because Young Me approached Logan in the field and kept him safe. Ah. So that's how suburban legends are made.

"Come on, Cat, you know that was the summer

Ben broke up with you for Cathy, and you started dating Jimmy." She thinks about that a minute, then slaps me at the back of the head.

"Ouch! Gram! I've had a heart attack here!"

Gram starts to chuckle and gives me a quick peck on the cheek. "Sorry, can't help it. It's a natural reflex, whenever I think about your years with Jimmy. Stupidest thing you did, letting him control you like he did. Your first broken heart led you to a shattered one. I was proud of you when you kicked him out, though."

I kicked him out? Huh. Good job. It took a do-over, but I finally did it right.

"At least she got us out of the deal," I hear my eldest daughter's voice, turn my head toward her, and grin when I see Jenna and her sister standing in the doorway, beautiful as ever. They're wearing coloured skinny jeans and short sweaters, but what makes them most stunning to me is they're beaming. At me.

"Good news, Mom," Alyssa rushes to my side and gives me a hug. "The doctors say you can leave tomorrow afternoon!"

"You're going to have to take some meds, several times a day, and exercise, but not as intensely as you were doing at The Cat Walk, okay? The doctor will explain it all to you today." Jenna takes my hand, and Alyssa grins at me. I notice she's wearing Jenna's favourite pink hoop earrings. Huh. They must be getting along well for that kind of loan to happen.

"The Cat Walk…" I quickly put together that's the name of my gym. "Sure. Sure. Er, you sure you girls aren't embarrassed by my, um, Cat Walk?" I turn to Alyssa.

"Of course not! It's so cool, what you do." Lyssa's her bouncy, energetic self, but something's different. She's looking me in the eye. That's pride. I see pride.

How did I get here? Did I actually have a heart attack while starting my Wii program? But Logan and Ben are alive and well. I've lost the weight, or possibly, never gained it, because I never felt the need to eat my way out of my guilt.

The changes could only mean one thing. Gene. Gene did exist. He did help me. We did fall in love. Madly, passionately in love, in a castle in Mornas.

So, where, or when, the hell is he?

17

I'm standing in the living room of our childhood home, secretly wishing Gram would stop what she is doing, pull up a chair, and bitch about society with me, like she used to.

"Those days are long gone. Now, she bitches on television." I chuckle out loud. A cameraman peers up from above his massive camera and winks at me.

"Right, you stay right there, that's exactly where we want you," he tells me.

I'm about to do a Public Service Announcement on Heart Attacks in Women with Gram, in the home from where she bases her wonderfully ridiculous reality show, Badass Grandma. I've concluded that this is all my fault, because she approached MTV with the idea for the show in 2004, when my marriage fell apart, and I needed money. It took a few years for the show to get rolling, but once it did, it was like an overnight success. Gram wouldn't have had the show idea at all had Gene and I not paid her a visit in 1993. Me and my big ideas.

After I left the hospital, memories of my new reality began moving in on my old ones. They didn't completely take over; at first, they were like a polite new housemate. As my heart healed, the new memories trickled into my consciousness like an IV drip, and as the days passed, they went from a slow drip to a steady flood. They never completely replaced memories of the accident, or of Ben and Logan dying. They simply helped cover the more painful memory abrasions, like a bandage. I still carried the scar tissue of my past underneath.

Some of the strongest new memories were of how Gram stepped up to the plate and took care of me after I left Jimmy. She wanted me to be able to afford a place, far away from the home I'd tried to make with Jimmy and the girls. She even encouraged me to go back to school to get my business degree. Thanks to her help with the girls, and her loan, which I've almost paid off, I was able to return to school in the evenings, get my degree in three years, and realize my dream of owning a business. The Cat Walk, our town's most-popular gym and day spa, is the culmination of many days of planning, and many nights spent brainstorming with Gram and my girls.

"Just a PSA, right?" I say to the camera. I have an

ear bud in, and someone in my ear is constantly giving me directions. I'll call him Won't-Shut-Up-Walt. "You're not going to film me for her show? You won't visit me at 'The Cat Walk?'"

"We can't do that, remember? Your Gram put a clause in her contract. The show doesn't involve any family members. Just her, and her friends and boyfriends," Won't-Shut-Up-Walt explains.

"Boyfriends? The woman is *ninety-one*!" I laugh.

Upon hearing this, another crew guy comes up to me and shows me his iPad. He's scrolling down Gram's Twitter account, @BadAssGrandma. She has 3 Million followers! "She pretends she doesn't have boyfriends," Crew Guy chuckles, "because it makes her more popular with the older men, I think, and leaves her open to make more jokes. Here, see this one? One of my favourites."

"Eww," I don't really want to imagine Gram with a boyfriend, let alone *boyfriends*, but I do firmly believe that real love is ageless, and timeless. Look at me and Gene.

I peer over the iPad and read the joke:

@BadAssGrandma: I don't really need a man no more. I just put Bengay in inappropriate places. ~Jan. 14th from Web.

I laugh out loud, just as Gram joins us 'on set.' She's in a made to measure, camouflage-print, velour jogging suit. I study the way she's standing; the way she's smiling at the camera crew. She's so comfortable in this new existence. It's not like she has changed that much. Sure, they've glammed her up a little, and she doesn't require a cane like before – but I think she's happy being heard, for once. She had all these fabulous, deep ideas when Cici and I were growing up, but she was already in her seventies. No one was listening to her; sometimes, not even her granddaughters.

Today, she's not bogged down by all my problems, either. She had told me time and again that I wasn't a burden to her, but living with a depressed, overweight woman and her teen daughters when she herself had fatigue, aches, and pains couldn't have been a picnic. I miss living with Gram. It was fun having her just down the hall from my bedroom, even though I didn't get as much privacy as I do now.

Now I have a fantastic room with an ensuite, and Alyssa has more than enough space in her room, with Jenna moving out, but money certainly hasn't bought us everything. It hasn't bought us time with Gram. These days, she's so busy with her reality show. She even directs episodes! How can one direct one's self in depicting their real life? I'd like to know. I desperately needed life direction for nearly 38 years! Only in this last year have I finally been able to direct myself in the right direction with assistance from a kind, sexy genie.

Was my time with Gene truly reality, though, or fantasy, or a dream, or all of those things combined?

I guess I'll never know. It's been 98 days since I last saw Gene. I miss him like sunshine on cloudy days. I miss him like a warm blanket on a cold Sunday morning in bed. I miss him in my bed. Mind you, we'd only truly mastered straw. I've tried hard to forget him, but how can I? I would have followed him anywhere, to any time, but, no, he had to go and save my life.

I've looked for him, of course, in as much as you can look for a genie. One night, when the girls were over at their cousins' house and I knew no one would catch me in the act, I opened up the old Wii in that box I'd stashed away in the hall closet. I don't really have free time to play Wii now that I'm running 'The Cat Walk', plus, I like doing the elliptical machine every morning. But I remember I felt like a kid on Christmas morning as I opened that box and pulled out the magical object that finally brought me real love.

———————

I NOTICE the Wii machine is quite dusty, and as I place it under the TV and hook it up to give it a try, I can't help wondering if Gene is allowed to take me on as his Master one more time. He has to successfully help one more person to be set free. Why not me? I still have lots of problems. Big problems. I'm practically screaming with problems. Singing them to the world!

"I need a genie! I'm holding out for a genie 'til the morning light!"

Oh Cat, don't do a Top-40-Tom. Just. Don't do it. You can't even sing on key.

No, no, I'm really feeling it, and the girls aren't here. I'm also in a black, form fitting spandex ensemble with matching headband, so I look almost like a Spice Girl or Britnaaay, Biatch, or well, okay none of them, not even close, but I feel sexy, and this is happening. Sorry, neighbours.

I jump up and start crooning to my beautiful white condo walls.

As I sing 'Larger than Life,' I belt it out louder than the other lines, hoping Gene will hear.

Please hear, Gene. Please show up. Please, I need you.

The hallway is still echoing with my voice. I'm standing there in the centre of the living room, arms wide open, waiting for something big to happen, but nothing does. After about three minutes, I fall down to my knees, and push the Wii off the TV stand. It comes crashing down, but it doesn't break. Instead, it puts a dent in my new hardwood floor.

Figures. You always were a FuckUp Genie. But I miss you. I miss you!

I don't allow myself to cry this time. Too many tears spilled over too many men.

He's not coming back.

"Okay, people, quiet on set, we're ready... and... action."

I never imagined I'd be doing this, in my childhood home, of all places. However, if it can save even one woman from what I went through when I had my heart attack, it's worth my time. So when Gram approached me about doing a PSA, I agreed without hesitation. She said it will air for a month or more, just before her show comes on every night.

"You are not Superwoman. You can't do it all," Gram beings her speech. The camera is focused on her in a close-up. "Maybe your parents told you that when you were growing up, but they were full of shit. You are not 'everything.' You need others to help you accomplish things. And if you start to feel pain in your chest, dizziness, and shortness of breath, honey, it's probably not gas. It's probably not 'nothing,' as you so often call it. It could be serious. It could be the start of a heart attack. Don't brush it off. Don't be an idiot!"

"Listen to your body. Listen to my Badass Grandma. Know the signs of a heart attack. It could save your life," I say the line I've spent hours memorizing, hoping I didn't slur any words. As I step away from the lights, I glance over at a monitor and see myself in it. *Not bad. I feel pretty good about my performance, and how I look. Would you look at that? So long, Ledusa, Goddess of Self-Loathing. I've finally conquered you. I've finally won.*

"That's a wrap! Ladies, that was perfect." Won't-Shut-Up-Walt has come out from wherever he was hiding, and takes the ear bud out of my ear.

"That's it? Gee, Gram, your job is so easy," I kid, and I notice someone from makeup has already swooped in to touch up her foundation.

"Yeah well, this is where your brush with reality ends, and mine begins, Fantasy Girl." She chuckles. Of course I'd told Gram all about Gene, how could I not? I didn't tell the girls or anyone else – it would just mess with our new reality – but Gram had met him, so I wondered if she'd remember him in our new time. Sadly, she didn't remember anything about his visit, including the two times she beat him up. She doesn't remember our old life. She believes my story, though, with all her heart, and loves to tease me about when, or if, he's ever coming back.

"You heard from Lover Boy yet? Don't worry about it. He's probably in the White House right now, catering to his recent Master, the President of the USA. That's why their country is such a mess. Your genie's on the case."

"Gram, be nice." I give her a goodbye hug, deciding then and there not to let on how upset I am over the loss. What can she do? It's not like we can put out a Missing Person's on a genie. I change the topic. "So, how are you going to mess with reality today?"

"Oh, nuttin' much. Directing the episode today,

though. You know, cupcake, I still don't really know what I'm doing there," she pauses for a moment. "I'm sure it's a lot like sex, and I'll figure out if I like it when it's over."

She never fails to crack me up. "Bye, Gram, good luck with that. See you at supper?" I blow her a kiss, and head for my car, feeling a lump in my throat when I remember the limo. It's not a limo, and Gene won't be there. He won't be sliding over to make room for me. I need to forget about him.

Just as I'm opening my car door, a familiar voice calls my name. I close the door and look up.

"Cat? Wow. Look at you! You look so healthy. That's great."

It's Ben. Real, live, living Ben is standing before me, and three Ben look-alikes are unsuccessfully hiding behind him. I lean against the car for support.

"Wow, Ben, how are things?" I don't know what else to say. It's not like I can tell him how relieved I am that he's alive. It's not like I can explain how I've been tossed into a new existence – an existence that's the only reality he's ever known – while my heart still holds onto sad and beautiful old memories.

Ben comes closer and leans in for a hug, and I hug him back.

This feels good, but you still betrayed me. You left me when I was most vulnerable. I don't blame you for my marriage to Jimmy, but I wish you'd stayed my friend after you broke up with me. You hurt me, but I still needed you. If we'd stayed friends, I may not have made the mistakes I did.

Of course, I can't say any of this. I don't think it matters anymore. I'm on a different path now, and so is he. But, he came here to see me. It's a start. Maybe we can start fresh, today. One more in a string of fresh starts I've been granted this year.

"Gram talks a little about you on her show, so I heard about your heart attack. But you look good," he says, and I can tell by his face that he is genuinely concerned for me. Or is he? I thought I could read his face back when we were dating, but I suppose he was fooling me, intentionally or unintentionally. Water under the bridge now… I wonder who he married? Gram never told me.

A bright red maple leaf flutters above our heads and floats down to the leaf-covered grass at our feet. I love this time of year; you can almost smell that back-to-school sense of change in the air, apple cider and mulling spices on the stove, pumpkin patch visits, wet woolen sweaters and scarves. And changes, all kinds of changes. Jenna is packing up the last few items from her room today, as she's met a nice new friend in one of her classes at Ottawa U, and they're moving into an apartment together downtown. Thanks to Skype and texting, we won't ever be out of touch for long, but she's promised to come home every few weekends for a family meal with me, Alyssa and Gram.

It suddenly occurs to me that I never had the chance to share this season with Gene. We only shared the Spring. I close up my long, dress-like cardigan and cross my arms to break the wind, wishing I could replicate the feeling of Gene's arms wrapped around me. It felt like coming home.

"Yeah, I'm doing the exercises the doctors prescribed and feeling a whole lot better than I did that first week," I say, hoping to change the subject. "So who are these little guys?" I ask, gesturing to the three boys, who look about four years old, and have just flung themselves into a wrestling match in a pile of leaves they've collected on the grass.

"Mike, Monty, and Mitch." He rolls his eyes. "Their M names were my wife's idea. I kind of had to go along since, you know, she was having triplets, and in the 8th month she wanted to murder me for impregnating her." He laughs. "What are the odds—" He interrupts to call out to them, "Boys, don't be so rough with each other!"

He looks directly at me again. "Cat, you know I married Angie, right? Angie, from our gang back in '93?"

"Oh, Angie, no, didn't realize that. I thought maybe," I take a breath. Should I say it? Sure. Get it out there. "I thought, maybe Cathy…"

"No. No, we dated but, no. She wasn't right for me." He looks me in the eye, like he wants to say something else, but he doesn't. Instead he puts his hands in his jeans pockets and looks at his running shoes.

"Well, we came here to get an autograph from Gram. We won some special 'backstage passes' on the Internet. I can't believe I know someone famous from when I was growing up!" He laughs.

"Yeah, she's a peach to live with now. She only wants the blue M and M's in her dressing room."

"Seriously?"

"It's a joke, Ben. A joke. Remember how we used to joke?" I say in a near-whisper.

"I do. I do. They were good times. Real good. I'm sorry I… I wasn't as responsible as I should have been back then." There it is. That's all I'll get. But it's good enough. I want to cry and give him a big, squishy hug. Instead, I give him a smile.

"Growing up isn't easy. We all make mistakes. I'm just glad I got to grow up with you, Ben, to see you live to have these three beautiful boys." I'm trying not to make myself cry, but it's coming. I take my sleeve and wipe my eyes fast, hoping Ben won't notice. He does, but he doesn't appear to think the tears are strange. He seems a little misty himself. He tries to compose himself by changing the topic.

"Did you read about Jake Hampton? He's back in prison. Aggravated assault. And Cathy?"

"What? I knew about Jake but, what… Cathy's in trouble?"

"Tax evasion." He rubs the stubble on his jaw.

"She always was the sly one, huh? Yeah, her fashion business is in real trouble now. Didn't you read last week's business section? It's serious. She may do jail time."

"God, we have *so* much to be proud of, GO Class of '93!" I laugh. He shakes his head and joins me in my laughter. I can't say I'm not feeling just a tad gleeful that Cathy has gotten kicked in the butt by karma. I hope her crime doesn't affect, or even destroy, her and her family, but I'm sure it will. I imagine visiting her in prison, just to show her I can bury the hatchet. Then I imagine making faces at her through that Plexiglas window, flipping through magazines, showing her all the new fall fashions she can't buy. Yeah, not sure I'm mature enough to pay her a nice visit. I'll have to work on that one. You can't grow *that* much just because one genie pays you a visit. I'm still a work in progress. I chuckle out loud, but Ben thinks I'm still laughing about our Disaster Class.

"And your business is doing fantastic, I hear. I have a bunch of friends with memberships. I'm proud of you, Cat. I always knew you were a star."

I have to catch my breath. I think I want to ask him and his wife to dinner, but I'm not sure how. As I try to find the words, one of Ben's kids - I know his name starts with M – runs up and tugs on his pant leg.

"Can we go now, Daddy? This is boring."

The boy runs back to his brothers and tackles them both again, so they're rolling on the grass once more. Ben calls out to him, "Okay, Mitch, just one sec…"

"Little boys…" He smiles at me. "What can you do?"

Then he takes my hand in his, as if to give it a handshake, but he simply holds it there for a few seconds. "Cat. It was so great to see you again. You take care." He gives me a quick wave as he gathers up his leaf-covered brood and walks with them toward Gram's house-set.

"You too, Ben. Take care," I call back, grinning and blinking back tears.

TIME TO MEET my girls for lunch at Herb's Café, and after that, we're going out for ice cream.

With sprinkles? Ah, I can remember Gene asking me this, so clearly. He was trying to distract me so I could tackle that castle wall, and I did. We did.

Yes, love, always with sprinkles. Always with hope. Always. I won't stop hoping.

I get in the car, put on my seatbelt, turn the ignition, and pull away from the curb.

I don't look back. I've done enough looking back.

It's time to look forward.

EPILOGUE

WHEN I ARRIVE AT THE FIRST TRAFFIC LIGHT, I STOP the car and look at the passenger seat where I'd put my purse, thinking I should grab my cell phone and text the girls that I'm running late. That's when I notice something different on the passenger seat.

Red roses, wrapped in pale yellow gossamer ribbon, little white date tag still intact. The bouquet sits in the afternoon sun, looking as fresh, and smelling as fragrant as it did at the castle in 2017. I pick it up and give it a whiff. No, I'm not imagining things. It's real. I read the small, typed print more closely. I was, after all, a bit panicked last time I was holding this bouquet.

K & E ~ May 4, 2017.

Could it be?

When I turn the date tag over, I notice some small handwriting:

> *I think this actually belongs to you.*
> *I'm so sorry I can't return it in person... yet.*
>
> *~ G.*

To Be Continued!

Don't miss Remarkably Great for the conclusion to Cat and Gene's adventures.

HUGS

From the 2015 edition

(Acknowledgements is so formal)

I have so many people to thank for helping me get this novel written, published, and out into the world.

To my parents, Linda and Barry, who encouraged my love of story-telling from an early age, and to my sister Jenn, for happily sharing a room with a yacky story-telling younger sister, and later, proudly sharing all my writing-related news on Facebook. I love you all.

To Bill and Finn, for never complaining about my last-minute (or "self-serve") dinners and my many moods as I tried to get the story written. Finn, one day when you're much older, I hope you read this book and that I finally move up on your "Funny Meter."

To Larry, for asking for 'More pages! More pages!' after reading the first two chapters in one sitting, and Elisa, for encouraging me every step of the way and helping me write the kick-ass query letter that landed me the contract; and to The Lodge Gals, for asking to hear the original plot and telling me what parts they loved & what parts needed more wine (wait, that's not what they said…); to Bill's family, Craig, Katie, Emily, Steph, KC, Julie Gross, Julie Gedeon, Heather P., Karen, Patty, Dave, Sarah, Ken & Maryanne, George, Beth, Caroline, Alison P., Andrea, Kim B., Kimberly F., Kimberley B., Saghar, Mel, Peter, Joe, Mark, Ron, Marcia & Mike, for helping me believe in this novel, and all my writing projects.

Finally, thanks to the ladies at Morning Rain Publishing! Your tagline says you're prettier than the average publisher, and I think you're way more fun, too. Thanks for all your hard work on this book.

Hugs for all!

HGS

March 2025

Wow, the last ten years has been a wild ride I never expected!

Thank you friends, family, followers. I can't believe I'm still working at this nutty, roller coaster of a career. And, for the most part, loving it! It's been a dream come true. I have you to thank for it.

What's next? Get ready to take *The Love Leap!* It's

another time travel rom-com adventure, but this one will take us to the Scottish Highlands, present-day and 1645.

You can preorder it at the link at my website (heathergracestewart.com) now to get the ebook at half price! before it launches on June 30. The print books will be available at this site shortly as well, and early reviews are most appreciated:

Buy Directly from Heather!

Books.by/heathergracestewart

Thanks for the advance support!

Love, Heather

ABOUT THE AUTHOR

Heather Grace Stewart is an award-winning Montréal poet and journalist who writes fast-paced, humorous, magical romance novels. *The Ticket*, a romantic comedy inspired by a true story, became an International Kindle bestseller.

Heather is the author of 23 works. She's reached over 360,000 readers worldwide via downloads, borrows and e-book, paperback, and audiobook sales, and all seven novels have been published by Tantor Audio or Dreamscape Media as audiobooks. In October 2020, *The Ticket* was translated into French. It was optioned by Passage Pictures in 2022. In October 2021, Polish rights to five of her novels were sold, and her books were translated into Polish audiobooks and e-books with the publisher Empik.

After receiving her BA (Honours) in Canadian Studies at Queen's University in Kingston, Ontario, Heather attended Montréal's Concordia University for a graduate diploma in Journalism. She worked as chief reporter of a local paper and associate editor of the national magazines *Harrowsmith Country Life*, *Equinox*, and *Canadian Wildlife* before starting her own freelance writing and editing business, Graceful Publications, in 1999.

In her free time, Heather loves to spend time with her husband and their young adult who's in college, take photos, practice yoga, inline skate, garden, cook, dance like nobody's watching, and sample craft beer —usually not at the same time.

Also by this Author

Remarkably Great (sequel to Strangely, Incredibly Good)

The Ticket

Good Nights

Lauren from Last Night

Lucky

The Love Leap (June 2025)

And more!

Visit heathergracestewart.com to browse Heather's complete book catalogue.